This issue is the hot summer wind that dries your tears. We wait in the shade of the red rock, hoping there is still water in the soil. We fear to dig, but we must, because there are sprouts to be rescued. This issue contains stories about the bonds of family (for both good and ill), stories about the changes that come over us as the seasons shift, and stories about how we decide to linger.

This issue isn't what you think it is, but, then, they rarely are . . .

Underland Arcana is published on a seasonal basis. This issue is published in conjunction with the summer solstice, when the hot winds descend and the birds fly backwards.

EDITOR
Mark Teppo

COVER IMAGE
Tanya / stock.adobe.com

SIGIL ART
Andrew Penn Romine

PUBLISHER
Underland Press
Clackamas, OR, USA

At night, the heat lightning flashes but does not drive away the shadows . . .

https://www.underlandarcana.com

UNDERLAND
ARCANA

~ 10 ~

Underland Press

Contents

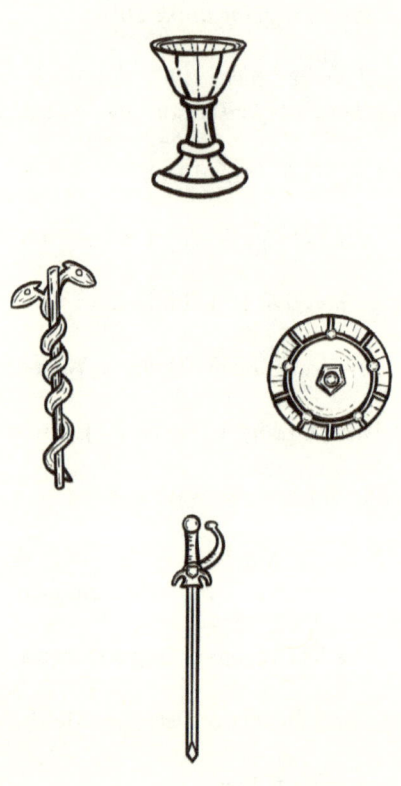

Digging in the Dirt

One of the reoccurring motifs in magico-religious structures is the cycle of death, burial, and renewal. It's right there in the natural course of our daily lives, after all. At the end of the day, we fling ourselves into bed, eager to be rid of the day. Eager to embrace oblivion for a few hours. Eager for a reset and a chance to start again. Seasonally, we see the new buds breach in the spring, and they grow tall and bear fruit during the summer. Then, in a rush, we harvest this bounty and hope it will sustain us through the death of the year. Over and again. Always and forever. Amen.

This cycle is there in the Wheel of Fortune card of the Tarot. Kings are born. Kings rise up. Kings fall down, to be buried again. Everything grows old and becomes mulch for the next iteration.

The other night, in passing, someone said: "No one gets out of this life alive." One of those truisms that you expect to see at the start of a chapter in a Frank Herbert book. "Water is wet." "Fear is the mind-killer." "No one gets out of this life alive."

There's a grim fatality lurking in these aphorisms. It's easy to slip into Eeyore voice when you reflect on them. "Oh, dear, what's the point of it all?"

It's a goddamn drag to carry this weight around. Trying to hold back the wheel is exhausting. None of us are strong enough anyway, and, perhaps, we're fighting the wrong fight.

The Wheel of Fortune is the tenth card in the Major Arcana. The ninth card is The Hermit, who symbolizes the internal and external reflection. The eleventh card is Justice, which is the weighing of the aspects. The twelfth is The Hanged Man, the realized mind waiting to be born again. And the next card is Death—the transformation and rebirth. Perhaps, when we focus on the Wheel, we're forgetting its place within the broader canvas of existence.

In April, I was asked to be on a panel at Norwescon, celebrating Greg Bear, who passed away late last year. The morning of that panel, as I thought over the stories I might tell about Mr. Bear, I learned that Rachel Pollack had passed. They were two writers who, in different ways, were strong influences. Bear, by being an irascible lover of language and a man with a persistent curiosity about the world; Pollack, by opening up my mind to the permutations and exaltations of the tarot. Both would agree, I think, that the bigger picture is the more interesting picture, and the little details are, well, subject to change at any moment.

I had wanted to talk about renewal in the editorial for this issue, but I'm talking about death instead. Though, perhaps, that is the proper way of things. The wheel turns, after all.

Mark Teppo
May 12th, 2023

Rachel Pollack: An Appreciation

It's worth saying that the current incarnation of Underland Press wouldn't exist without Rachel Pollack. Back in the day, I knew her as the writer who followed Grant Morrison on *Doom Patrol*—a job that was like jumping off a cliff over a lake of fire with lead weights strapped to your ankles. And yet, Rachel managed to make the series her own.

After her run (which lasted for several years), she wrote a few novels which were well-received and which were recognized by several awards: *Unquenchable Fire* won the Arthur C. Clarke Award in 1989; *Godmother Night*, the World Fantasy Award in 1997, as well as being nominated for the James Tiptree Jr. Award and the Lambda Literary Award for Transgender Literature; and *Temporary Agency* was nominated for a Nebula Award and the Mythopoeic Award in 1995.

She disappeared from novel writing for a few decades, but then returned in 2014 with a young adult novel called *The Child Eater*. And lastly, there's *The Fissure King*, which was one of the first books I acquired when I took over Underland Press.

Rachel, you see, had written a novelette about an occult detective named Jack Shade. It was called "Jack Shade in the Forest of Souls." It appeared in *The Magazine of Fantasy & Science Fiction*, and a year later, it was followed by "The Queen of Eyes."

It was about this time that I reached out and politely asked of her plans for Jack Shade. "If there are going to be more stories about him, I'd like to chat about doing a bind-up." She replied that it wasn't something she had thought about, but yes, if that was an option, she had an idea about how to bring his story full-circle. We agreed on this plan, and she offered an exclusive Jack Shade story that would bring everything together.

I waited. "Johnny Rev" appeared in *F & SF* in 2015. "Homecoming" followed in the Jan/Feb 2017 issue the same magazine. All that was left was the final story, and once I had it in hand, we had a "novel in five parts."

The Fissure King was published in late 2017. It is, in my opinion, one of the most delightfully layered occult detective novels ever written, and I'm perpetually thrilled that it's an Underland Press book.\

But it's not just *The Fissure King* that made a mark on the press. There's also the influence of the tarot.

The first anthology was *XIII*—the thirteenth title Underland Press did overall, and my first title as the new publisher. Death, in the tarot, is about transformations. About the change that is wrought by the process of shedding skins, being reborn, and finding our way back from deep caverns. We followed that anthology with *XVIII*, a collection of stories influenced by the Moon.

Which brings us to what you hold in your hand: *Underland Arcana*, a regular fiction magazine where the tarot is reflected again and again in the stories. When I sit down to select the tarot card for each story, the book I always reach for is Rachel's *78 Degrees of Wisdom*, her guide to the meaning of the individual cards.

One of the first "fancy" tarot decks I bought was the deluxe edition of the *Vertigo Tarot*, the project she and Dave McKean did for DC back in the day. She wrote the text for the book, and McKean worked DC characters into his illustrations for each of the seventy-eight cards. I scanned each card, cleaned them up, and had them running as my computer screensaver for years. The Celtic Cross readings I did for the characters in my first novel, Lightbreaker, were all done with the Vertigo deck.

I'm sure this explains so much about my career.

Rachel passed on April 7th of this year. Her spirit persists in every issue of *Underland Arcana*. With this issue, we're breaking one of the unspoken rules about the project by using an image for the cover that is clearly a tarot card. This is the High Priestess—she who knows the secrets and who waits for us to be wise enough to ask the right questions.

You'll Never Believe What this Norse Monster Did to Keep His Mother Out of His Man Cave

~ Sarina Dorie

My nefarious cronies and I had been waiting for Ragnarok to come for ages and it still wasn't here, so we figured the best way to pass time was to enjoy ourselves at least. I sat down to play cards with Jarl the Ogre and Bjorne the Troll. Aarne the Fenrir Wolf couldn't join us for our monthly poker match because it was a full moon and he tended to go a little crazy, even for the likes of us monsters.

Jarl nodded to his cup of watered-down ale. "Hey, bro, you got anything stronger than this?" His leathery gray fingers held his hand of cards. His beady eyes darted about. I knew exactly what he was looking for.

I glanced over my shoulder at the torchlight casting flickering shadows over the walls of my underground lair. The coast was clear. I heaved the jug of mead out from where I'd hidden it under my chair and poured us drinks. Jarl took out the tub of special brownies, and by special, I mean the ones with the fermented shark in them. Yum!

"So, about those humans that keep attacking us," I said between bites. "Don't you think it's time we stand united and get rid of that ass-hat, Heorot?"

Jarl belched and patted his ashen belly. "My dad says we should ignore bullies and their childish attacks. Sticks and stones, you know, bro?"

Bjorne gulped down his mead and poured himself another. "The thing is, Gee, I don't care, so long as they don't kill anymore demon-licious monster babes. There's a scarce commodity of them as it is."

I shook my head. "You two have your priorities in the wrong places."

Bjorne barked out a laugh. "Whatever. Not everyone can satisfy their sexual appetites with a sock fetish."

"Shut up! You're high on hákarl again, aren't you?" I munched on another brownie. Pretty soon I would be high too if the night went according to plan. "You two really are bad influences."

"Complement accepted, bro!" Jarl poured another drink.

We were on our third round of mead and just starting to have fun when—wouldn't you know it?— my mom slithered in. Part she-giant and part sea monster, she loomed nearly as high as the stalactites on the ceiling. I took after her in size, though I didn't know where I got the horns, hairy posterior or bulging eyes. I was a big-boned, handsome devil—wherever those features came from—and the terror of all Denmark.

Bjorne's jaw dropped as he ogled my mother.

I elbowed him. "What's your problem?"

Jarl wisely tucked away the brownies.

Mom dusted one set of scaly hands across her polka-dot apron and carried the vacuum in the other set. She crouched to pick up a sock from the floor and held it away from herself, glaring at it with disdain. "Pumpkin, please don't leave your socks on the floor like that. I just found three of them in the adjoining cavern and one in here. I can't understand why you insist on—"

My face must have turned purple in humiliation. I nodded toward my friends, trying to make her understand she was interrupting.

She stopped, her vexed expression changing once she saw my friends. "Oh, gentle demons, I apologize, I didn't realize we had company. Just pretend I'm not here." My mother tucked the dirty sock into a pocket and vacuumed around us. I slipped the jug of mead back under my chair and arranged my abundance of leg hair to hide it from view. She was such a teetotaler. She'd probably dump it into the swamp if she caught a whiff.

"Sorry," I mumbled, some of my big, bad monster persona slipping. "She'll move on to a different chamber soon and then we can have some real fun."

"This is what you get for living in your mom's basement, bro," Jarl said.

I glanced at my mother. She hadn't seemed to hear over the roar of the vacuum.

Bjorne clapped me on the shoulder with a hulking, hairy hand. "What? That's your mom? Dude, introduce me! She's so hot!"

I stood so fast my chair toppled over. "If you ever say that again, I will uncoil my wrath and get all Ragnarok on your ass."

"No need to get your panties bunched up, man. I just think she looks kind of like, well, you know. . . ." Bjorne winked at my mother, who was now dusting stalagmites.

My mother giggled. The sound grated on my ears. Didn't she realize how embarrassing it was when she flirted with my friends?

"No, I don't know," I said. "And I don't want to know."

Bjorne and Jarl exchanged glances. Bjorne whispered, a decibel that was only slightly under his shout. "You know, like that pin-up girl in the centerfold of my magazine."

"Well, she isn't!" I pounded on the table hard enough that some of the poker chips flew off. One of them rolled across the cavern floor, stopping when it smacked into my mother's webbed feet.

She stopped dusting. "Gee, are you playing what I think you're playing? After our last talk about gambling?"

"Mom, chill. It's just a game. It's not like we're playing for human heads or anything." We only did that at Aarne's house.

She pursed her lips. "By the way, I was cleaning your room and let the humans out from their cages. They were really making the place stink to Valhalla."

"Mom! How could you? They're just going to go back to Heorot and stage another attack on us. I needed those captives to take over Denmark."

"That's nice, dear." My mother shrugged her immense shoulders. "I guess you'll just have to capture some more tomorrow. After you muck out the swamp and mow the lake weed." Her gaze shifted from my horn-covered face to my shaggy leg hair draped over my chair. I followed her gaze. The jug of mead. I pushed it further into the shadows.

Mom pursed her lips. "Is that what I think it is? You know you're too young for that."

"Mom, I'm over a thousand years old."

"This is totally lame." Jarl threw down his cards and stood. "I'm going to Aarne's lair. I don't care if he tries to rip my face off because it's his time of the month."

My mom raised one of her many hands to wave goodbye. "Tell your mother I said hello, Jarly."

Jarl crossed his arms. "I don't have a mother."

"Oh, really? Then who did I run into at the monster suffrage meeting last week? Do demons just birth themselves? That is so like a male ego to think it can create the world all by itself."

By Thor's hammer! She was off on one of those tirades again. My day kept getting worse by the minute.

"Us, she-demons do have names, you know," she went on. "Just because humans aren't willing to write us down in their histories doesn't mean we are any less important than male monsters. I, for one, am sure I'll do something noteworthy to be recorded for all time."

This coming from the woman who fit the image of a Stepford wife.

Jarl edged closer to the exit. "Um, I'll tell my mom you said hi, Mrs. Borghild. Bye!"

Bjorne smiled, a lecherous gleam in his eyes I knew all too well from his exploits. He bellowed. "So where's your dad, bro?"

"By the powers of Asgard, she isn't a MILF," I growled under my breath. I prayed she hadn't heard.

As usual, Odin ignored my prayers.

"My husband? I ate him," Mom said with a shrug. "I guess I'm a real man-eater."

Of all the indignities, she had to bring that up again. When would it end? Couldn't she see she was ruining my life?

"You know, it really is empowering to be a liberated monster who permits herself the same appetites as male monsters. And by appetites, I'm not just talking about eating humans." She wagged a finger at Bjorne. Her smile was too cloying for my liking. Flirting with my friends was not allowed!

I cleared my throat. "Mother, could we get a little privacy? We're trying to have a guy's night."

"I'm sorry, dear. I didn't realize I was interrupting your big boy party. I should be getting back to the kitchen anyway. I tried to bake something from scratch and ended up summoning a demon instead. Now I've got a hot date cooking in the oven. A gingerbread golem." She feather-dusted her way out of the chamber.

I clenched and unclenched my fists, watching her go. I didn't think my day could get any worse. When I turned back to Bjorne, he was reading one of his dirty magazines. He opened the centerfold. A she-monster sprawled suggestively across the double page.

My jaw dropped.

There she was. My mom. Naked. Ick! I was going to be traumatized for the rest of eternity.

"I'm into golems. Do you think your mom would be into a threesome?" Bjorne asked.

Odin, have mercy! I thought I would die a thousand deaths right there. I was so grossed-out I puked up my mead and then passed out in a pile of my own vomit.

So there I was, alone in the underground lair, abandoned by my friends who had cooler places to be. I tried not to think about where Bjorne was. It made me nauseous when I thought about that son-of-a-troll and my mom.

I grabbed a club out of my trove of weaponry and headed to the kitchen, ready to pulverize my former friend. The only evidence they'd been there was a mess of gingerbread crumbs.

I couldn't even wallow in my misery in peace. The humans were at it again with their loud partying. The noise echoed from their stronghold above and into the swamp and our caverns. I usually didn't mind the ruckus, but today it reminded me of how alone I was—and how no one was around to party with.

Feeling grouchy and having nothing better to do, I decided to storm the humans' keep.

By the time I trudged through the swamp, passed a golf course, the row of fast food joints, and scaled the fortress walls, most of King Hrothgar's men were drunk and passed out in the great hall. They'd probably been celebrating the return of their escaped heroes after my mother let them out of their cages.

"Disgusting," I muttered, mostly because I could have been enjoying a similar state by now if my night had turned out differently. I considered stomping on the heads of the humans on the floor, killing them in their sleep. I was too depressed to bother.

A warrior stepped out of the shadows. He was tall, blond, and bearded like the rest of them. I couldn't tell if he was the king or someone else. These humans all looked the same to me.

"Ah, you must be Grendel. I've been searching for you," he said.

I crossed my arms. "You know, if you're going to throw a loud party, the unspoken rule is to invite the neighbors so they don't mind."

"I hear you have a problem with your mother. I might be able to assist."

Hope alighted in my heart. "By the power of Asgard, I'd give my right arm to be rid of her!"

A mischievous smile flashed across his face. He cracked his knuckles. "That can be arranged. Allow me to introduce myself. The name's Beowulf."

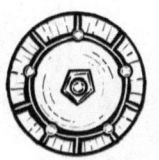

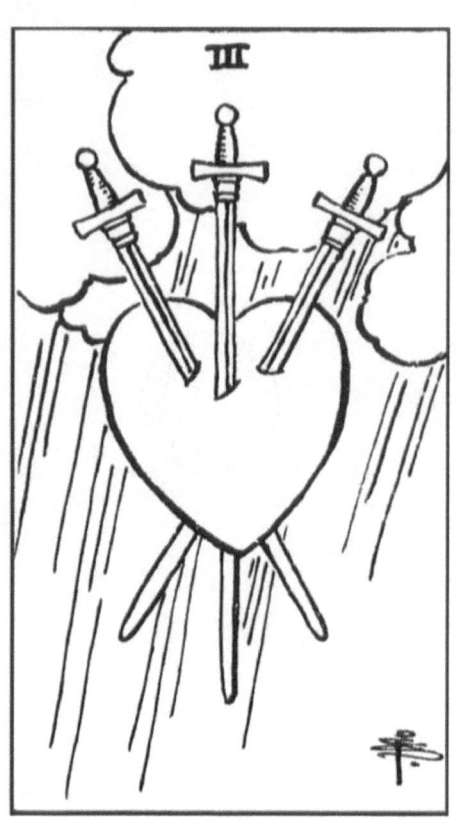

A Fiery Lull

~ Elad Haber

Dear Maria,

I set the field aflame. Again. Third time in three years.

First, it was locusts. They came from the south as a murmuration, huge and curved into the shape of an evil grin. They descended on my crops, ate and ate their bodyweights and more. I had no choice, but to burn them out. We surrounded the fields with flamethrowers, killing everything in our path, plant and bug, native and invader.

Next, it was the *federales*. They got wind of some of my unusual strains and were on their way to investigate. Like the insects before them, they swarmed in black vans, kicking up a dust-storm behind them. I gave the signal to burn the fields and even my precious incubator plants.

And now, it's the latest cartel war budding up against my business. I am not associated with any one family, so I'm in the middle of it, a victim of the violent winds that pass through the country like a traveling tropical storm.

We are packing up to leave to America. Etain is here with me. She misses you. You would be surprised at how big she's gotten! Even picking her up is getting difficult for this old man. She's holding the doll you gave her, with the red hair, like her momma when I first met you.

I turned your old studio into my office. Your artwork still hangs on the walls, the glazing glowing red from the fires. We're watching through the big windows as fieldhands burn my life's work.

I hope they are giving you my letters. Please know that though we are leaving the country, we will be back for you. When things quiet down. When it's safe.

I promise, Maria. I will come back for you.

Te amo, mi vida.

—Jorge.

(Scrawled across a billboard near East Hampton, NY)

TO SLEEP, PERCHANCE TO DREAM.

Yo bro! Check this out.

I was working a quad shift at the farm. You wouldn't even recognize the place. You worked a summer here, like, what, five years ago? We've got three huge greenhouses now. The boss named them after those famous ships, the Nina, the Pinta, and the—uh—I don't remember the last one. Besides, he doesn't let anyone in that one.

So, I'm doing my usual work: Assessing every new flowering plant, making notes about size and color. The rows are endless, green aisles like trees along a highway.

Small plants at the front and larger, thicker ones by the back. It takes me half a day to do one row.

Suddenly, there's a whisper beside me. I startle and almost drop my tablet.

"Hey," she says again.

It's the boss's daughter. You remember her, right? She was a little stick of a girl at fifteen. Well, she looks a lot different now. She had on a runner's outfit, a tight crop top and even tighter pants. Her legs seemed to go up to her chest and her hair was tied into a ponytail, it snaked down her back like a tattoo.

You know me, bro, I fall in love easily.

"Hi," I said.

She stepped further out of the shadows. She was wearing inky black so she still blended. She came close to me. "I need your help," she whispered.

"What—what can I do?" I stammered.

"I want to do something bad," she said.

I felt myself stiffen. Maybe love wasn't the right word.

She grasped my hand and started leading me away. "Um, but, I, uh, I have to work!" I protested for some stupid reason.

She just laughed and opened a nearby service door. "It's okay," she said, "I know your boss."

Outside, it was night, but stadium lights created an artificial day. As usual, the farm was abuzz with activity, but the other people were far away or engrossed in their duties.

The girl led me through the shadows of the bright light beyond the dome of the Nina to hug the walls of the Pinta.

I could hear the machinery in there, churning along 24/7. The flower was converted to other forms in there: heated oils, crystalline wax, or distilled liquids for tinctures.

"Where are we going?" I whispered.

"Come on!" she replied.

We were exposed for a few minutes while we ran towards the next greenhouse, the one marked S/M. She found another darkened corner and we were hidden again. The building looked bigger and more imposing up close. We were both breathing heavy from the run. She had a wild, expectant, look on her face.

She pressed a button and a door revealed itself from the blank wall. Then she punched in a code and the door hissed opened. She grasped my hand and pulled me forward. The door slid shut behind us.

Inside was a laboratory, of sorts. It was similar to the greenhouse where I worked, but even at a glance, I knew the flowers were different. The strains were - I'm not sure how to describe it - unique. There were alien-like purple flowers, stalks and buds that glowed neon green, a few were an unsettling dark blue, while others looked a natural green, but when I looked closer, they had thorns where they shouldn't or had strange colorful patterns.

"What is this place?" I asked, awed.

She took a moment to let it all sink in. "Experimental strains. My father's life's work."

I crashed landed back to reality. I started to back away. "I shouldn't be in here," I said. "We should go."

I turned away. That's when she kissed me.

"Julien," she said. I didn't know she knew my name. She made it sound exotic, European. "Please stay."

I swallowed and nodded. She smiled and leaned in for another kiss, a peck on my cheek. Then she turned on her heel and started wandering among the strange plants. At various places, random as far as I could tell, she picked off a flowering bud and then went back to searching. At one point, she went back and grabbed a bit more from two bright green plants with orange hairs.

Finally satisfied, she ducked away from the rows of plants to a kind of maintenance area. There was a ladder to a loft. She went up first. I tried not to stare.

The loft was small, but furnished. A couple of couches, a few screens mounted to the walls. A bookshelf.

She sat down on a couch and beckoned me to sit next to her. On the little table in front of the couch, she laid down the buds she had collected. Their multi-colored hues looked rainbow-eqsue. She used the bottom of her palm to start crushing the buds, mixing them together.

She broke the silence. "Have you heard of Lull?"

"No," I said quickly.

"Liar," she grinned.

I sighed. "I have heard of it, but it's dangerous. I think. Doesn't it make you . . ."

"Yes," she said. "Or so I've heard. I've never tried it before."

I had a bad feeling about all of this, but what was I supposed to do at this point?

I asked, "How do you make it?"

As she crushed more of the flower, she said, "It's a cocktail. A blend. Different strains, combined in the right amounts. I've been researching, for awhile. I think this should do it."

She finished crushing all the flower and started rolling a joint from the crumbs.

I gulped. "I don't know if I want to, you know, do that."

She laughed. "It's not for you. It's for me. I wanted someone else here to, I don't know, just to make sure nothing goes wrong."

"Like if you stop breathing or something?"

"Or something."

She used her tongue to seal the joint and took a moment to admire it. It was thick like a baby banana. She rummaged around the table until she found a lighter. She lit the joint, took a long drag, and sat back. Her eyes were closed already and she said in a kind of contemplative tone, "You ever just want it all to stop?"

And then she fell asleep.

☉

ZERO STARS!!

I rarely write reviews, but I feel compelled after your RUDE employees treated my friends and I like garbage last night.

It was my best friend's birthday. We arrived around 2 a.m., already tipsy from the drive over. As soon as the doors swooshed open, we were elated. The place was packed with beautiful people, dancers hovering in the sky, and those interactive projection things—I love those!

The hostess floated in to greet us looking like some kind of goddess. She wore a long flowing green dress, with a wide slit in the front, a little too much skin in my opinion, but she pulled it off. She introduced herself, but it was hard to hear over the pounding music. I think she said her name was Elaine.

Anyway, it started off great. As she took us through the winding pathways of the club to our table, maybe-Elaine smiled and chatted with my best friend. Projection-butterflies came at her command to rest on her manicured fingers. Then she pointed at one of us and the butterfly came to rest on our shoulders or top of our head.

But then things took a turn once we sat down. We ordered a few bottles, a few thousand dollars' worth, just to start! Then your hostess leaned in to me and tried to sell me some "designer cannabis strains."

I said, "Bitch, I don't smoke that street rat stank."

Well, I guess she didn't like that. Even though, what's that phrase, the customer is always right—especially the customer who just dropped a few thousand dollars.

As soon as I refused her under the table deal, she got rude and insulting. I saw her talking to some of the waitresses and looking in our direction. We were practically IGNORED all night and I know it was because of her.

I complained to the manager and I saw him talking to her later that night, there was shouting and some wild gesturing, although I couldn't hear what they were saying. I hope she got fired.

Even if she did, I won't be back to your club and neither will any of my friends until you hire NON-RUDE employees.

☉

(Spotted on a billboard outside Albany, NY)
WE WERE MEANT TO SLEEP.

Dear Maria,

I'm sorry it's been so long since my last letter.

I've never lied to you. So, I need to tell you, it's been tough, lately, with Etain.

She is unable to keep a job and she keeps getting into trouble in the city. As a teenager, she was rebellious and mischievous. I was the same way. Heaven knows I was a terror for my poor madre until I met you and settled down. I have tried to be understanding and forgiving with her, but she tests me. Whenever she is home, we fight. She blames me for her mother not being around. She is starting to hate me, I fear.

I don't know how much longer I can keep the lie from her.

In happier news, Etain has taken a liking to one of the field hands at the farm. He's not a lowlife like her usual boyfriends—he wouldn't be working for me if he was— but he has a big mouth. Always texting some brother who lives in another state. A little too chatty, in my opinion. But she seems happy.

Although she doesn't need the money, I have insisted that Etain hold a job in addition to her studies so she can learn responsibility, just like we did. She's still trying to find the right fit.

I will write again soon.

Te amo,

—Jorge.

☉

hey bro. I think I have a girlfriend. Etain, aka the Bosses'
Daughter, likes to hang around the employee's hut waiting
for my shifts to end. I get some weird looks from my co-
workers, but I don't care.

She usually looks like she is the middle of a workout,
all skin and sweat. But not tonight. She is wearing what
may have been a chiffon gown years ago, but full of rips
and tears, like a Halloween costume. Her hair was half-
done up one side and stringy and down on the other. Her
makeup was similarly half-done, as if she got bored with
the whole thing in the middle.

"Hi," I said when I saw her. She was sipping on a vape.
The clouds that surrounded her were a maelstrom of colors.
"You look nice. Are you going to a party?"

"We," she said grasping my hand like she does, "are going
to a party." She wrinkled her nose in that way that may
be considered rude to most people, but doesn't bother me.
"You'll need a shower and a change of clothes."

She smiled wide at the prospect and then took off at a
run towards the big house. I followed after her. The house
was massive and textured in glass. I'd never been inside the
house before, even after working here all these years.

It was, as expected, garish and loud. Artwork on every
wall, sculptures in every corner. Massive chairs flown in from
Northern Europe, it looked like they still had some snow on
them. I tried to stop, to gawk like a gallery-viewer, but Etain
yanked my arm and led me up the stairs to her suite.

She had three rooms all to herself, each one larger than the next. Her closet was the size of my apartment with seating and lighted mirrors.

"I grabbed some of my dad's old clothes, back when he was a bit . . ." she made a squeezing gesture with her hands. "Younger."

And then she laughed in such a cute way, I felt my heart pulse.

An hour later, I emerged wearing a button down shirt, slacks, and a belt that squeezed the life out of my stomach. We got high and then went downstairs to the waiting car.

In the backseat, on the drive to the city, Etain was calm, as always, but I was a ball of nerves.

"Are we going to be late?" I asked her.

She smiled and slid open a compartment between us. There was a grey satchel inside. She patted it like a dog.

"Hard to be late when we're bringing the party."

Oh.

She saw my discomfort. "Are you nervous?"

"A little."

"Don't be. It's . . . hard to describe. But wonderful, in its own way."

I remembered the lectures in health class. "Isn't it like death? Like you die for a few hours?"

She laughed. "Not at all! There are these amazing images. Like you are watching a movie of yourself. Or you are experiencing something from a different perspective."

"Different how?" I asked.

"You'll see."

She leaned back and sighed, as if she had already taken some of the Lull. I watched the rise and fall of her chest and lingered on the exposed bits of skin beneath the tattered dress. I was used to seeing her in more relaxed attire. Dressed up as she was, it was like she was a completely different person.

The car pulled up to a high rise and a doorman opened the door for us. I half expected paparazzi, but there was only the busy background chatter of the city.

Her heels clicked against the marble floor of the hallway as she led me towards an elevator. Not surprisingly, she pressed the button for the top floor.

The door opened directly into a penthouse apartment. There were floor to ceiling windows overlooking a bustling night-time metropolis. In the daytime, it's probably flooded with light. But tonight it's all shadows. Even the big chandeliers and floor scones are set to a dim. Sheets hang from the high ceiling, forcing us to push our way through the apartment as if we're under colorful water.

We emerged from the hall to a large living area. Guests, similarly dressed in finery, but somehow damaged or weathered a bit, called out to Etain. She manufactured a wide smile, the brightest I've ever seen on her, before she embraced them. She introduced me, but I didn't catch any of the names.

Etain unveiled the grey satchel from behind her back and the other guests tittered and smiled at her. The hostess, obvious in her pristine gown and impossible heels, separated herself from the gaggle. She fake-smiled at me and then leaned into Etain and whispered, "Wait till you see the Den."

We all followed her down another hall to a bedroom which looked like about the half size of one of the greenhouses. There were blankets and pillows piled up in mazes and cul-de-sacs. Beds lined the walls, more than I've ever seen in one place.

"It's perfect," Etain whispered. She was glowing, excited. I couldn't help it, I was excited too.

In the center of the room were three massive vaporizers. Etain went to study them. The little gaggle of women dispersed expect for the hostess, who hung back next to me. She was a foot taller than me in those heels.

"So you're the new boyfriend?" she said to me with a sidelong look. "Must be a special person to keep her interested."

There was malice in her tone. Something else, as well. She gave me a weak smile and walked over to Etain. She put her hands on Etain's waist and pulled her closer to her, an obviously intimate gesture. They both laughed.

I wandered the corners of the large room, smiling at the beautiful strangers. I overheard one woman lean into her friends and say, "I read some people used to do it in the middle of the day."

One of the ladies gasped. Another one exclaimed, "How uncouth!"

From the center of the room, the hostess called out, "Everyone find someplace comfortable."

There were more titterings and nervous whispers from the crowd. Etain swung the grey satchel around and started *loading the Lull into the vaporizers. They started to emit a mist into the room. It was thick and white like snow.*

Etain smiled at me before she was engulfed in the storm.

See you on the other side, bro.

Sleep

From Wikipedia, the free encyclopedia

This article is about sleep in humans. For other uses, see Sleep (disambiguation).

For centuries, mankind has relinquished half of their lives to somnolence. In the mid 21st century, spurred by the Accelerated Evolution Movement, or AEM, which was the scientific movement to reach humanity's evolutionary goals through technology and bio-engineering, sleep became a target. Politicians ran on a campaign of radical change. Without sleep, they argued, how much more could we accomplish? They poured billions in AEM research facilities until a "cure" was found. A combination of drugs delivered to five year old children through a year of micro-doses tweaked their bio-chemistry so that sleep became, after a single generation, eradicated. Some countries banned it completely while most societies frowned upon it, asking instead, What would you do if you had half of your life back?

[static]
"Dispatch, dispatch, reports of active blaze on 66th St.
and Amsterdam. Penthouse. Engines en route."
[static]

☉

(Photographed on a billboard near New Platz, NY)
I WISH I KNEW YOU.

Dear Maria,

There has been an incident.

Don't worry, Etain is fine. But some of her friends have died, including her boyfriend, Julien. There was a fire at a party they attended in Manhattan. Apparently, they were *sleeping* at the party. There was an open flame somehow that caught fire, we don't know how yet. The police have been around a few times now, asking questions. They seem to think Etain is responsible.

She didn't come home for days and then she appeared one night in my study.

Once I made sure she was fine, I demanded answers and asked her why the police were asking questions about her and her experience with *sleep*.

We had an argument. Our worst yet. She brought you up, accused me of taking away the only person who ever truly loved her.

I had no choice, I had to tell her the truth. About that day, in the old farmhouse, when she was a baby. About the fire you started.

I will never understand how you left her alone in the house. What would have happened if I came home a little later? I couldn't risk something like that happening again. I had no other choice.

I told Etain everything, finally.

Tears streamed from her eyes, but she was stone-faced, like polished steel.

"I don't believe you," she said.

"You're a liar!" she shouted.

I shouted something back.

Then she ran. Out of the room and out of the house. I don't know where she went or if she'll be back.

—Jorge.

☉

Official transcript of podcast "Mysteries of New York," Episode 16

[ominous musical intro]

SC: *Hello and welcome to the episode 16 of the "Mysteries of New York" podcast where we discuss mysterious occurrences in New York state. I'm your host, Samantha Cunning, with my co-host, Darius White. How are you doing today, Darius? Staying warm?*

DW: *Trying to, Sam, but it's not working. We're look-ing at single digit temps for the rest of the week here in Buffalo.*

SC: *Brr. Let's get right to today's topic. A topical one, a news story that is getting a lot of play throughout the national outlets.*

DW: *Although it is very much a New York kind of story, wouldn't you agree?*

SC: *Definitely, Darius. And what are we even talking about? The billboards, of course.*

DW: *Yes. The Poet of Poughkeepsie.*

SC: *So named because of the first spotting of the bill-board on a state road outside the city. We only have one picture of that sighting before county officials painted over it. The picture was taken in a foggy winter morning and obscured most of the text. But the style was unmistakable.*

DW: *Especially when similar fragments in thick black spray paint started showing up on the highways and roads of Long Island and then upstate. This was about six or seven months ago, isn't that right, Sam?*

SC: *Yeah, that sounds right. It was a news-worthy story almost immediately. There was a whole group of photographers who roamed the roads looking for new fragments.*

DW: *Before authorities could burn them down.*

SC: *That's right. A few weeks after the first fragment was painted over by local authorities', other mu-*

nicipalities around the state started doing the same thing. But after every washing over, the fragment would re-appear as if by magic. So, they started taking more violent action. Was it the same person, working tirelessly through the days and nights to re-do his or her work, or was it copycats, fans, or maybe it was some kind of collective?

DW: No one knows for sure, although there have been a lot of speculation about the Poet's identity and motivation.

SC: It was the substance of the words that angered the local governments. The fragments were about sleep. The joy of rest. The lost magic of dreams.

DW: We both can attest to years of demonization of sleep, first in school, then from politicians, business owners, etc.

SC: And that's what scared them.

DW: Yes. They burned the billboards so the fragments could not be redone. It was not uncommon to drive down a highway in New York and see a seemingly endless row of burning billboards.

SC: But who is the poet of Poughkeepsie and what are they after? What is their goal?

DW: We'll dig into that more after a short message from our sponsor.

☉

Maria,

They're allowing me one last letter. Maybe I should have called? We haven't spoken in so many years, I don't know if I even remember the sound of your voice.

I've been arrested on federal charges. It was Etain. She was using a cocktail of my strains to jerry-rig a sleep inducer. The FBI has hundreds of texts from Etain's boyfriend detailing how she manufactured the drug and brought it to the apartment where those kids died. Even if she didn't start the fire, they are blaming her for what happened.

I swear, I didn't know what she was doing. I would have stopped it if I knew.

Of course, the Feds don't believe me. They are sending me away. She'll be on her own now. Maybe she always was.

In the end, I was a liar. I never came back for you.

Good intentions too often turn into broken promises.

Lo siento, mi amor.

Goodbye, Maria.

$$\odot$$

r/newyorkstate—Posted by u/SheDidn'tDoIt six days ago

[MEGATHREAD] FRAGMENTS

okay, guys, this is it! I've asked the mods to close down all the other sightings threads so we can keep it all in one place.

It won't be long now. State police have closed down all roads and exits out of the state. Federal authorities are going door to door. New York is locked down and it's going to stay that way until the Poet is caught.

It's our last chance to help her get her message out. With the enhanced scrutiny, sightings have been rare, but they're out there. Billboards are being monitored so we're starting to see pieces of her last poem on motel signs, drive thru windows, behind Costco's, in gas station bathroom mirrors, wherever they are, WE HAVE TO FIND THEM.

Remember: Every drawing has a nearby number. Put those numbers in sequence and we have the order. Then it's just a matter of finding all the fragments. Good luck, guys!

EDIT #1: We are over halfway there!

EDIT #2: Have you guys gotten any weird home visits lately? Like, from the FBI? At first I thought it was prank, but then they got all mad at me when I wouldn't let them in. They threatened to arrest me, but then I let them search my house and they were satisfied, I guess? They said they might be back.

EDIT #3: I think we should stop.

☉

(Published on the front page of *The New York Times*)

When I sleep,
I dream of my mother.
My mother I never knew.
My mother who tried to kill me.
Flames
Have followed me my entire life.
When I close my eyes,
I let them take me.

Burn me this time.
I'm ready.

Noblesse Oblige

~ *Frances Lu-Pai Ippolito*

Your face was ashen when you first peeked over the lid at me. So sweaty too. I didn't mean to scare you. Go ahead, pull up a chair. Take a seat. Catch your breath.

Let me guess: when they said "cheap seats" at the Apricot Pavilion, you thought you'd get the ugly, fat girls. Or the old ones, so ancient they'd be nothing but loose skin draped over spoiling meat. You didn't expect . . . well what did you expect?

I don't get out of this tank much, but I was young once, more alive than now and I remember (there's a lot of time in here to remember) how it works on the other side of the wall. You came into the Lobby and there were red lights and beaded curtains, and the girls lined up in a beautiful parade. And each one stroked your arm as you walked by. Said "hello," told you her name, offered a tour, and asked if you'd like to talk in private and sample the session you could buy.

But you strode past the ladies to the beechwood bar. Was Lao Wen in the Hawaiian shirt still there? It's been a while. I hope so. Lao Wen was perpetual like a rock—his chubby ass always planted on the high vinyl stool behind the bar. By the way, I loved that stool. I used to sit there as a kid when I came to visit my father's business. Did you notice Captain America's face on the stool under Wen's butt? He bought it from Arnie's Arcade in the building next door. That was before the rioters burned that whole building down.

Anyway, where was I? Sorry Hon, the mind wanders from the body a lot these days. What'd you think of Lao Wen? When I knew him, he drank a lot, didn't shave, and blew gray smoke rings toward the ladies. No doubt he has that lazy right eye and the jeans that don't cover the sideways smiling rear split. But don't be mistaken; Lao Wen looks slow, but he's no joke. Did you see what he's stored behind the desk? Did he show you his dictionary? The man doesn't read. It's a safety deposit box where he keeps pieces and bits of the people he doesn't like in last name alphabetical order.

At the bar, you must have leaned over to whisper "Noblesse Oblige" into Lao Wen's ear. (His ears are gross, right? Untrimmed hairs turned spider legs crawling out the holes.) Being Lao Wen, he wouldn't have blinked (he's seen a lot), but his good eye may have widened just a bit. There are, after all, only two types willing to order off the secret menu: the destitute or the depraved.

I think . . . you're definitely the former. In fact, you remind me a bit of someone I dated in college. Sweet, quiet, and gentle. He wanted to marry me. We never went all the way. But I think you'll treat me real tender and considerate. Not like the others who regularly visit; they're very mean. Just because I'm used to it, doesn't mean there's no pain. I can feel it, especially when someone wants it to hurt.

You, though, have nice brown eyes. Yes, I'm almost looking forward to spending time with you.

I bet Wen-Wen gave the usual warning in that raspy baritone of his. "Contrary to Reddit threads, these visits aren't free. We charge your account and collect the balance later." Then he pulled out the contract—thick and dense with ant-sized text. You signed. He offered you a drink as part of the house package and let you in.

When the room door opened, I watched you from the domed mirror bolted to the ceiling above my tank (some clients like that angle). You were shown the light switches and the tank keys hanging from a hook on the wall. "Two hours is enough," you said to someone who closed the door. The tank keys fell when you first tried to take them off the hook. Your hands shook and I heard you whisper encouragement to yourself. You dropped the keys a second time when you tried to unlock the partially frosted glass lid. The keys jingled like wind chimes when they fell onto the polished concrete floors. You picked them up and tried again (and again) and eventually (about four minutes and twenty-three seconds later) found a way to put the keys in—three keys inserted all at once, all turned to the right to release the seal. Once the lid lifted, the tank lights flooded on and you screamed.

Without skin, people really do look the same. Red muscle strung over sticks of bone, bangles and dangles of flesh, marbled balls of fat, and sinewed ropes and ties that bind it all together into a cramped chassis caged by bones. I've had a lot of time to think and it finally all makes sense. The inside's rainbow of pink, veiny blue, and even dabs of chartreuse are all colors spelled lowercase. But the colors on the outsides are spelled with Capitals that cause people to close ranks. Black, Red, Yellow, Brown, White, or whichever race, it doesn't matter beneath that largest organ covering our hidden bodies. Peel back the husk to reveal the universal truth: we were all grown and birthed from a mother's womb. A true gospel of sorts. The Gospel of the Flayed.

And you've come to pray.

Do you like older women? Benjamin Franklin said you should: "When women cease to be handsome, they study to be good. To maintain their Influence over men, they supply the diminution of beauty by an augmentation of utility."

I was very old when they skinned me. I won't tell you how old because a man should never ask a lady her age. And, sweetie, without any wrinkles I doubt you can figure it out. I will say, however, that we older women are always full of use. Service—small and great, and love— soft and amiable, especially for a young one in need. Just like Benny said, "There is hardly such a thing to be found as an old Woman who is not a good Woman."

You look twenty. Could this be . . . your first time? No wonder you look like a shivering kitten. Shy and skittish like my college love. Gosh, that was so long ago. Maybe even a hundred years? Right before all the women began to die from the disease. Daddy knew early what was coming. And when Mommy died, he pulled me from school and locked me in my room. (Cream walls, a shelf with a single book by Benjamin Franklin, and two twin beds. One bed covered in Barbie dolls. I loved those dolls until I hated them. Gave them names, pretended they were real people—married, pregnant, divorced, and then dead.)

Daddy fully sterilized the room. Never let me out. (Sixty steps wide by one hundred steps long—I know because I doublechecked and counted the steps all day long.)

He had the money to keep me safe. Built on the backs of the women you passed on earlier. And you'd think when the world lost 75% of its women that the brothels would close and everyone would protect the remaining ones that lived. But Daddy only got richer. Sure, he had to close a few locations from staffing shortages. Though overall, he had plenty to keep the bars on my windows tight and to pay for the security of our home and his business assets. Plus, he let some of the women have kids—only girls, of course, because the world didn't need any more men. The daughters that survived were offered employment, overtime, and extended benefits.

I never agreed with his management or business practices. We were rich and well-off and Daddy should have shared. So few women left to go around. So few to mother the children and take care of the men. It simply wasn't fair. I was never very good at school, but THIS I knew I could do. THIS I could give. Wasn't it my duty? But Daddy never left me alone, never wavered from keeping me *safe*. "'He that lies down with Dogs, shall rise up with fleas.' I promised your Mother before she died," he said over and over on the other side of my reinforced door, like she would have wanted me caged.

Then Daddy *finally* died. I'm ashamed to say I was excited.

Freedom, I believed. I wasn't young anymore, but before I lost my hair and skin, I was pretty. It's hard to see, but examine my skull, the curve of the lower jawline, the perfectly rounded top of my head, and the smooth path of muscle grains on my face. The buccinator, the muscle around my lips, is particularly strong and well-developed; in college, I was a good kisser.

It's hard to remember sometimes that I haven't always laid in state within this heated glass box, on this platform, in this lacy negligee with the name "Sleeping Beauty" etched on a brass plaque nailed to a wall. (By the way, I feel you fingering the hem of my skirt. You're hesitating. Don't worry, they wash it and me after each use.)

Oh, but I digressed. Daddy was dead, but no one would let me out, no matter how I begged, cried, or threatened to kill myself. It's all because of the fine print in another kind of contract, Daddy's Last Will and Testament. The lawyers explained women, like possessions or chattel, required protection, and the Executor couldn't set me free and violate his fiduciary duty per the signed and binding agreement. "Too dangerous. No telling what a mob of wild men would do if they knew about you. A woman is safest in the home surrounded by a wall of protecting men."

So I remained contained in that secured, air-filtered room until one day, it was my turn to die the privileged death of a geriatric age. The lawyers came back. This time I read the fine print. This time I forced them to amend the clauses. This time there was nothing they could say for I was the last of the family; I had outlived them all.

When I donated my body to science, I failed to, perhaps, take into account where I might end up. I imagined a training hospital for pre-meds, a history museum of female anatomy, or even the skeletal exhibit in an elementary classroom (I always liked children). But when I was carted away to the mortuary, I realized that the outside air smelled and tasted of burnt things, that the roads were bumpier than decades before, and that much advancement had been made in the preservation of women's bodies.

In a mortuary room of steel walls and no windows, there were a pair of gowned men with latex gloves snapped on.

"Good, we got this one before she was completely brain dead," one said to the other.

"Advanced age. Body is in excellent condition."

"It's a pity about the skin and hair. Imagine what she'd be if we were able to preserve them."

"Yes. . . do you think that we could—"

"You mean before we start the process?"

"Yeah, the body is nearly perfect. All the limbs and digits intact. She even has all her teeth."

"But off the record, right? And only if I get to go first."

"Sure, Bob, you're technically my boss anyway. Not like she's going to tell on us."

They laughed and unzipped their pants. That was "technically" my first time. And though I was almost dead, it stung when they broke through the parts of me that had never been employed; the nerves alive enough to feel the service I delivered.

After my first time, the men preserved me. Filled me up with cocktails of I.V. fluids that transformed me from flesh to forever. Unfortunately, the process didn't, as you see, preserve the skin and hair. Those dissolved. The rest though, including my mind, is maintained in all its plasticity.

I know you can't actually hear me. I've tried to move, to communicate—say things, scream, cry, anything to let people know I'm still here; not just a silent, broken doll for you to hold. But no one knows.

Anyway, back to us, enough about me. I like you. I hope you don't mind me sharing and thinking all these things at you. This is *our* first time and we are about to become close friends.

Oh! Be careful! Don't fall! Climb slowly into the tank, my friend. The contract you signed with Lao Wen absolves the Pavilion of all liability. No one will pay if you get hurt. An assumption of risk. Though I want you to know this is more than an arm's length transaction for me.

You're looking away, avoiding my face. I wish I could stroke your hair, pat that bare chest, and see myself in your eyes. Am I a gorgeous nightmare? Even so, I know you want me, need me. Sweetie, that's alright. I'm here to give. I hope you don't mind that I pretend you're the one I was forced to leave behind.

Oh, good idea! Turn off the lights!

As the wise Benny Franky once said, "In the dark all Cats are gray."

After Image

~ H. L. Fullerton

I'm staring at a photo of B— when I first notice the floater. I mistake it for a smudge on the photograph and let out a cry of dismay. Then I realize there is something wrong with my right eye.

Thank god it's not B—'s picture. I have so few. Only the two I nicked from the impromptu shrine at Cavali's and the blurry one on my camera phone. I blink rapidly— flutter, flutter, flutter—and my vision clears. But of course, I don't realize this is a haunting until later.

I met B— while we were both working at Cavali's—me at my laptop, him as a barista. Working from home sounds grand, but spending all your time within the same four walls gets claustrophobic. You hunger for contact with the outside world so I lugged my laptop from coffee shop to sandwich bar, any eatery equipped with Wi-Fi that didn't mind me hogging a table for hours on end. Instead of calling myself a telecommuter, I dubbed myself a laptop nomad. I stopped roaming once my eyes landed on B—. Cavali's became my oasis and I spent less time staring at my screen and more time glancing at my desert prince.

There's something so electric about the young, as if all their pent up life radiates their tight, smooth pores. I never noticed it when I was that age, but now I am drawn to twenty-somethings in a way I can't explain. The older I get, the more attractive, the more alive, they become. And B—, well, in his black apron over white shirt and dark jeans, he captivated me. His deep set Valentino eyes, green, crinkled when he smiled, which was often, and he had dark mussed hair that cascaded across his forehead. To hide his widow's peak, he once told me, because his mother believed it to be bad fortune. I've heard she blames it for his early death.

I never stalked B—, never once followed him home from Cavali's. But from ten till three I surreptitiously feasted on him whenever he was in sight. My greedy eyes traced the fall of his hair, the almost delicate curve of his ear, the angle of his jaw, the nonchalant way he'd relax against the counter. I thought my staring harmless and even when he fell ill, I didn't stop. Just noted the sallowness of his skin, the bleary eyes and the change in his step; switched to fantasies where I nursed him back to health.

One morning when he brought me a refill without me signaling for it—one of the many reasons I adored him—I ventured, "You don't look so hot. Late night?"

He smiled. "I wish. No, I think I'm coming down with something. I just feel off, you know? Like something's missing." His hand tapped his chest, then fell to his side. I suggested a B-12 shot, wished him well and sipped my coffee. Closing my eyes, I replayed the scene on my eyelids, rewrote some of the dialogue, and let myself be carried away by the aroma of Cavali's dark roast and the memory of his slurry-sounding voice.

No one is sure how he died. Rumors say his doctors are still puzzled over the whole thing. But I have a theory. I think . . . I think it was me and that is why the floaters happened. In my defense, I didn't know what I was doing. My mother always said it wasn't polite to stare, but she never told me it was dangerous.

I'd never even heard of floaters until my vision started periodically blurring. Fuzzy dots blotted out letters on my computer screen, hid numbers and caused me to rub, rub, rub my eyes until the dots disappeared. Then the headaches began. I blamed computer fatigue, grief, the dim lighting of Cavali's and relocated to a brightly lit, chain coffee place. The baristas' green aprons in this new locale were sharp reminders of eyes I once avidly watched and their constant teenage chatter—*he was like* and *I was like* and *that is soooo*—grated my nerves. I found their brew bitter and swore they roasted their beans with napalm. And the floaters still danced in my eyes.

My eyes started playing new tricks on me. Movement in the corner of my eye would signal B—! to my brain and I'd whip my head in that direction only to find no one there. Coming out of the 'customers only' bathroom one day, I caught sight of B— at the end of the short hallway, leaning against the café au lait colored wall. Wearing his black Cavali apron. He was smiling at me.

I stopped, blinked in shock and glanced again. My vision dissolved into floaters. When I reached the end of the hall, I passed a bald, paunchy man whom I couldn't have mistaken for B—. He eyed me with suspicion, I must have stared too hard, and hurried past. I checked my urge to take another gander, forcing my eyes to the table where my coat was slung over a chair back. I never returned to that particular establishment and renewed my round robin of Wi-Fi hot spots.

My troubles persisted. I made an appointment with an eye doctor. I told him about the floaters, the blurred vision, my headaches. I did not mention seeing a dead barista. They ran tests. I have a slight astigmatism, he told me. I might need glasses. No, doctor, I need more than that. Focus is not my problem. There is a dead person flitting in and out of my peripheral vision. Can you do something about that?

I went back to Cavali's last week and saw B— lounging against the counter, one elbow cocked on its top, a smile simmering on his rosy lips. I smiled back before I remembered he was dead and couldn't possibly be standing there. I gave my head a small shake as if to reset my brain.

When I looked again he still stood there, same position, same welcoming grin frozen on his face. I blinked and kept blinking, but he didn't disappear. He didn't move either and the smile I so adored turned sinister in its rictus.

Grief, I told myself, *it's just grief.* Spotting a dead loved one is not uncommon. Our minds see what they want to see and here in Cavali's I expect to see B—, therefore I see him. I shouldn't have come back, no matter how horrible the coffee is elsewhere.

I averted my eyes from B—, kept them at half-mast and shuffled in line until I was next. "Can I help you?" the barista said. I made eye-contact and inhaled sharply. The lounging, smiling B— stood before me in vivid color. Unnerved, I dropped my gaze to my hands. They quaked. "Are you all right?" the voice said and it wasn't B—'s; it had the flat cadence of some mid-west city.

"Yes, yes," I spluttered. "Caramel macchiato, heavy on the cream." I glanced at my server. B—'s insouciant image overlapped him, as if my mind had combined past and present into a double exposure for my eyes to puzzle over. I slammed my eyes shut and, in case B— didn't disappear, averted them while I paid and received my drink. Then I sat at my favorite table, careful not to gaze towards the counter. But B—'s presence crowded me and I left without even checking my email.

I almost wish the floaters would come back. Instead of my vision blurring and clearing, I see the faint outline of

B— in that same lounging pose—one elbow akimbo, hair falling into his eyes—superimposed on the sides of buses, etched onto trees, twisting the features of everyone I pass into grotesques. No matter how much I blink, I can't banish him from my sight. In fact, his outline is filling in, becoming more substantial. There is color in his cheeks, I can make out his sweet smile, yet he is still a cardboard cutout of himself. But real, so real that sometimes I think I could reach out and touch him.

This strange double vision causes migraines. I draw curtains, pull shades till my apartment is black and still he colors everything I see—and it's getting worse. Sometimes when I close my eyes, his haloed silhouette is tattooed on my lids.

People tend to think of eyes as cameras, capturing every detail, photographing every moment, snap, snap, snap. Like the optic nerve is a USB cable plugged into your brain, filing away these images for playback or printing at a later date. But that's wrong.

Eyes act more like a television set streaming images. Some are too fast to catch, some linger when you power off, etch-a-sketching the last image until it fades to black.

The wife of a colleague of mine ruined his plasma screen when she paused mid-way through a movie to take a phone call, then forgot she forgot about the movie and went out grocery shopping. By the time he found the paused television, Colin Farrell's face was burned into the screen. He joked, "Some fucker gets the Virgin Mary on a dollar fifty tortilla and I've got the goddamn shroud of Colin Farrell on a eight thousand dollar piece of equipment. Why couldn't she have left it on *The Last Temptation of Christ* instead of *Alexander*."

That after image on electronics? It's called a ghosting.

It's difficult to get anything done when someone constantly interferes with your sight. I squint a lot and people keep telling me to get glasses. I don't think glasses can solve my problem. I do, however, buy a pair of sunglasses and wear them all the time. Now people aren't privy to my eyeball gymnastics as I strain to see where I am going or who I am talking to or what I am looking at.

I keep hoping he'll go away. Go haunt someone else.

But what if he doesn't? What if this isn't my subconscious screwing with me, but something else? I don't think too closely about what that something else might be. But . . .

There are cultures that believe you steal a person's soul when you photograph them. What if my greedy eyes and all their secret staring stole something from B—? He'd said he felt like something was missing and still I ate him up. Staring at a person, day after day, maybe that captures them bit by bit by bit. Maybe that is why we say things like: *the eyes are the windows to the soul* and *out of sight, out of mind* and *seeing is believing* and *what're you lookin' at?* and *Mom! Johnny's staring at me.* Maybe in our collective consciousness we realize that there is a danger in all this eyeballing, that it can go too far and baristas can end up dead and imprinted on our retinas.

Or maybe that's just me.

I watch TV and pretend that B— is burned into its screen inside of my lenses. I know I'm only fooling myself, but I'm okay with that. Unexpected movement makes me sit up on my couch. I didn't turn my head yet B— moved. He appears to be standing straighter, mimicking the actor in the show. I switch off the TV and stare at the white wall across from me so I can be sure of what I'm seeing.

B—'s arms fold across his chest. He turns to face me, full on. "Like what you see?" he asks and I can feel his breath on my ear even though he appears to be six feet away. He throws his head back and laughs.

My heart seizes. My hands clutch at the bottle near my feet. I pour liquor down my throat. *It's the alcohol,* I tell myself. *That's all. You're hallucinating.*

"You're not wasted," B— whispers and his voice slinks down my ear and coils around my cochlea setting off tiny shudders. He takes off his black Cavali apron, leaving him in a white button-down shirt, rolled up to his elbows, and a well-fitting pair of jeans. He undoes a few shirt buttons.

Uh-oh, I think.

"Isn't this what you wanted?" There is menace in his tone.

I shake my head and squeeze my eyes tight, trying to shut him out. He says, "Oh, no. It's too late for that." My eyelids are filled with his green, green eyes, so close, hideously close. Weight presses down on me, as if someone has sat in my lap. I feel myself pushed back into the cushions and struggle to stand, but he's right, it's too late.

Something soft brushes my cheek and I start to sob. "Shhhh," he says. "We'll have plenty of time for crying later. Open your eyes and look at me. The way you used to."

I claw at my eyes.

I am in the supermarket throwing items into my cart. I can't read the labels and B— is refusing to help. I can smell the coffee three aisles over and it nauseates me. B— flicks his finger at me and a stinging sensation burns my mostly good eye. I twitch and curse. Rub the burning eye until the pressure builds as if the whole thing might pop free of my skull. Then my hand is pulled away from my face. B—, who is crystal clear against rows of streaky colors I take for shelves of canned goods, says, "Permanently blinding yourself won't help."

An old woman toddles over to me. I can smell the Jean Nate powder and the urine soaked into her Depends. She is a floating blob behind a smirking B—. "Is there something wrong with your eyes?" She reaches into her voluminous handbag and rummages. "I have drops."

I wave her off, thrust my cart forward. I bump into a display. Packages hit the floor. I'm fine. Everything's fine. There's just a ghost in my eye.

Many Deaths Before Dying

~ *Warren Benedetto*

The empty lot next to Eddie's house was the football field where Joe Montana threw the game-winning touchdown to Jerry Rice. It was the baseball diamond where Mark McGwire beat Jose Canseco in the most epic Wiffle ball home run derby in MLB history. It was where Rambo took down the Predator with a Nerf gun, and where RoboCop blew the Terminator's head off with a Super Soaker. It was my favorite place to hang out with my three best friends.

And it was the last place I saw them alive.

The four of us had known each other since we were toddlers. We lived in the same neighborhood, went to the same schools, and played on the same Little League teams. Eddie's house was our main hang-out spot, partially because of the empty lot next door, but also because his mom kept the best assortment of Tastykakes stocked in the pantry. Even better, his house had a big finished basement with a ping pong table and a Nintendo with its own dedicated TV. He had all the best games, too: *Mike Tyson's Punch-Out, Metroid, Double Dragon,*

Warren Benedetto

Contra. He even had *The Legend of Zelda*, the one with the shiny gold cartridge that I coveted so much.

The lot was nothing special, but that's also what made it so special. It could be anything we wanted—a sports field, a war zone, an alien planet, or whatever else our imaginations could conjure. Some of my earliest, fondest memories were of the four of us running around in that lot, having squirt gun battles in the summer and snowball fights in the winter, then retreating to Eddie's house for Elio's Pizza and Fanta Orange Soda.

The lot was mostly dirt, about the shape of a football field, with a row of dark green hedges separating it from the neighbor's yard. The ground turned into a mud pit when it rained, but it hadn't rained in weeks. That's why we were so confused about the enormous puddle that had appeared there overnight. There were no sprinklers, fire hydrants, or water mains nearby. The nearest hose was coiled up way over by Eddie's front porch—it was nowhere near long enough to create a puddle in that part of the lot. And yet, inexplicably, there it was: a perfectly round circle of water, maybe fifteen feet across, with a mirror-like sheen that reflected the cloudless sky overhead.

"You're telling me you have no idea where it came from?" Marco asked Eddie.

"Dude, I swear." Eddie held up his fingers in a *Scout's Honor* gesture. "Jack, tell him."

I nodded. "Yep. We were inside all night."

The previous evening, the four of us had been out in the lot until well after sunset, tossing a baseball around while listening to my Def Leppard cassettes on Eddie's boombox. We only stopped once it was too dark to see the ball anymore. Marco and Shah went home, but I spent the night at Eddie's, watching Indiana Jones movies on his VCR until 2:00 A.M. We were together the whole time.

"This sucks," Marco complained. "Now what do we do?"

The plan had been for us to play Wiffle ball all afternoon, but the puddle was directly in the middle of our infield, in the exact spot where the pitcher's mound was supposed to be. It was so big that it even encroached on the base lines we had scratched into the dirt with the heels of our sneakers the day before.

"We could run around it," Shah suggested.

"Or through it," Eddie added. "We'll just take our shoes off."

I peered at the puddle, trying to examine it from different angles. "I don't know, guys. Looks pretty deep."

There was something about the thing that just felt *off* to me. The puddles in the lot were usually muddy and brown; the water in this one was perfectly reflective and oddly still, with a surface unbroken by mosquitoes or water striders. That was unusual—any standing water in our area was usually a breeding ground for insects. But not this one. It was like someone had left a giant compact disc in the middle of the dirt, shiny side up.

"It can't be *that* deep," Marco said. "It's a puddle, not a lake."

"Why's it so shiny then?"

"Don't ask me. Ask Mr. Wizard." Marco pointed at Shah.

Shah Patel was the resident genius of our friend group. While Marco, Eddie, and I spent most of our free time playing video games, Shah preferred hacking into government computer systems using his dad's dial-up modem. He couldn't *actually* hack in—he had no idea what he was doing—but that didn't stop him from running up exorbitant long-distance phone bills while he tried. His favorite movies were *War Games* and *The Manhattan Project*: he was a real "let's steal plutonium and make a nuclear bomb for the Science Fair" kind of kid.

"Hold this." Shah handed me the yellow plastic Wiffle ball bat he was carrying, then squatted next to the puddle to get a closer look. "Hmm. You sure it's even water?"

"What else would it be?"

Shah sniffed the air then wrinkled his nose. "Not sure. Smells like—"

"Your asshole," Marco interjected.

"You would know," Shah shot back.

Shah wasn't wrong about the stench. I couldn't vouch for whether it smelled like his asshole or not, but it didn't smell like water. It had a noxious odor that reminded me of Mr. Birnbaum's chemistry lab: a mix of sulfur, ammonia, and . . . something else. Something sour.

Shah tapped his finger on his lips thoughtfully. "Maybe it's mercury."

"Like from a thermometer?" Eddie asked. "Where the hell would that come from?"

"A meteor."

"I'm pretty sure we would've heard a meteor hitting the ground next to my house, Shah."

"Hey," Marco said, pointing at the Wiffle ball I held in my hand. "Lemme borrow that for a sec."

"No. Why?"

"Just give it."

Marco tried to snatch the ball away from me, but I dodged out of the way. Instead of reaching for the ball again, he feigned a blow to my groin—the kid was a notorious nut-flicker. I immediately reacted, dropping the Wiffle ball and lowering my hands to protect my crotch. Luckily for my testicles, it was just a ruse, but it had achieved the intended result.

Marco snatched the ball off the ground and tossed it into the water. It landed right in the middle of the puddle. There was no splash. No ripple. It didn't bob or bounce. It hit the surface of the puddle and just . . . stopped. It was like someone had pressed pause on the VCR at the exact second the ball had touched the water. Then, ever so slowly, the ball sunk. That was strange too—it was made of hollow plastic. It should have floated. But it didn't.

"Whoa. That was weird, right?" Shah looked at us to gauge our reactions. "It's like some kind of non-Newtonian fluid."

Marco nodded thoughtfully. "Mm-hmm. Yep. That's what I was thinking too." He clearly had no idea what the hell Shah was talking about.

"Now what do we do?" I said to Marco.

"About what?" he replied innocently.

"About the ball!"

"Just go get it."

"And reach it how?"

"With the bat."

I looked at the yellow plastic bat in my hand. It was about three feet long, nowhere near long enough to reach the ball from where we stood. "It's not long enough, dumbass."

"That's what she said."

"Why don't you just walk in?" Eddie asked.

"Why don't *you* just walk in?" I snapped.

"Use the bat," Shah suggested. "See how far down it goes."

"You do it." I held out the bat to Shah.

"Oh my *God*," Marco groaned. "You're such a pussy." He grabbed the bat away from me. "Gimme that."

My face flushed with a mixture of embarrassment and anger. Kids our age called each other pussies all the time, but I always took it personally. I couldn't help it. None of the other kids had a Dad who was an actual goddamned war hero like mine was. He had saved like fifteen guys in his unit in Vietnam, taking out an entire enemy encampment while getting riddled with bullets and shrapnel, then carrying the wounded one at a time back to the LZ to be airlifted to safety. He had two Purple Hearts, a Bronze Star, a Congressional Medal of Honor . . . he even met President Nixon. My dad would never call me a pussy—he was way too old-fashioned to ever use a word like that—but I always felt like, deep down, he must be thinking I was. I listened to music by guys who dressed like girls. I was more into books than sports.

I didn't like to hunt, fish, or do any of the things that he did with his dad when he was my age. Hell, I was almost a teenager and I was still afraid of the dark. I would never be half the man that he was, and I knew it. I think he did too.

Marco plunged the bat into the puddle to test the depth, sinking it as far as he could without getting wet. "Damn, that's actually really deep," he said as he swirled it around. "I can't even feel the bottom."

"Just like your Mom," I grumbled under my breath.

He pulled the bat from the water and shook it dry. "Ha ha. So funny I forgot to laugh."

"Maybe it's, like, an old well or something," Shah said. "Or a sinkhole."

"That would suck," Eddie replied. "So much for ever playing Wiffle ball again. Or anything else."

Marco handed the bat back to me. A wicked grin formed on his lips. "Dare you to jump in."

"Yeah, right."

"What's the matter? You scared?"

"No. Are *you*?"

Eddie began untying the laces of his Reeboks. "I'll do it."

"See?" Marco said. He clapped Eddie on the back like a proud father. "Eddie's not a pussy."

"Stop it," I growled through clenched teeth.

"Stop what?"

"I'm not a pussy."

"Okay. So, prove it."

I didn't move. I didn't say anything. My face felt like it was on fire.

After a few moments of waiting, Marco nodded. "That's what I thought. Pussy. Pussypussypussy—"

"Fuck you." I started to lunge at him, but Shah stepped between us and put a hand on my chest.

"Chill out, Jack. He's just kidding." He gave Marco a disapproving glare. "Right?"

"Right," Marco said. His tone was unconvincing.

While Marco and I were busy arguing, Eddie kicked away his sneakers and peeled off his socks, shorts, and t-shirt. He stood there in his tighty-whities, swinging his skinny arms as if loosening his shoulders for a swim. "Who else is with me?" he asked. Nobody else volunteered. "All right, then," he said with a smug grin. "See ya later, pussies!" He took off in a sprint toward the puddle and launched himself into the air, drawing his knees up to his chest for a full cannonball. "Kowabunga!"

I spun away and shielded my face in anticipation of a soaking splash of water. Marco and Shah did the same. But no splash came. Instead, there was a sharp slapping noise, the sound of an epic belly flop from a diving board. I turned back to the puddle to see Eddie sprawled on top of the water, staring at the sky with a shocked, pained expression on his face. It was like the water had turned to solid Jell-O when he hit it. Then, just like the Wiffle ball, he began to sink. His arms flailed as the seemingly-solid surface suddenly liquified underneath him. An abbreviated scream escaped his lips before it was cut off by water flooding his mouth. And then he was gone.

Marco squealed with laughter. "Holy shit, that was epic!"

Shah bent closer to the puddle, trying to see past the reflective surface. He looked up at us, his brow furrowed with concern. "Think he's okay?"

"Relax," Marco said, his laughter tapering off. "He'll come back up."

We waited for what was probably ten seconds, but it seemed like forever. Finally, I broke the silence. "He's not—" My voice caught in my throat. I swallowed hard, then continued. "He's not coming up."

"He will," Marco answered. "Eddie!" he yelled. "Come on, man! Quit screwing around!" He laughed again, but I could hear panic fraying his voice.

Shah snatched the bat away from me and thrust it into the puddle. "Eddie!" he called. "Grab on!" He moved it around, trying to find Eddie's grip. "Come on, dude! Grab the bat!"

"Do you feel anything?" I asked. My heart was pounding in my chest. I had a very bad feeling about what was happening.

Shah plunged the bat even deeper, submerging his arm up to the shoulder. "Nothing," he grunted, his voice straining. "He's not—"

Suddenly, Shah was jerked violently forward, plunging face-first into the puddle. His legs kicked wildly at the dirt as he was dragged into the water. Despite his struggling, there was no splashing, no splattering—it happened as silently and smoothly as if he had slipped into a pool of shadow. The puddle barely even rippled.

Marco stared at the spot where Shah just had been.

"Guys?" His previous bravado had evaporated. He sounded scared. "Guys, come on."

"We need to get help," I said quietly. But I didn't move. I felt rooted in place, as if my feet had bonded to the Earth's crust. I was frozen solid, utterly paralyzed with fear. Shah hadn't just fallen into the puddle. He had been *pulled*. By what, though? The only thing I could think of was an alligator. But were there alligators in our part of New Jersey? And even if there were, how had they gotten into the puddle? And where had the puddle come from in the first place? And why was the water so deep, and so weird? None of it made any sense.

"Shit!" Marco cried. "What do we *do*?" I didn't respond. "What do we do?" he asked again, his voice rising with panic. When I still didn't answer, he looked back at Eddie's house, searching for some sort of solution. His eyes lit up. "The hose! Let's go, gimme some help!" He pulled me by the arm, finally breaking me from my trance. I ran after him as he sprinted across Eddie's yard to where a long green garden hose was coiled up beside the front porch. "Pick it up!" he ordered.

I began gathering heavy loops in my arms as Marco unscrewed the hose from the pipe. Once it was free, we carried the messy tangle of rubber over to the puddle. Marco sat on the ground and began wrapping one end of the hose around his ankle.

"What're you gonna do?" I asked.

"I'm going in." He twisted the hose into a knot and pulled it tight.

"No!" I felt tears welling in my eyes. "You can't."

"You want them to drown?"

"No, but—"

"Then help me!" He limped to the edge of the puddle, dragging the heavy rubber hose behind him. "Count to twenty. If I don't come up by then, pull me out." Before I could protest any further, he took a deep breath and stepped into the water. He dropped like a lead weight, instantly vanishing under the mirrored surface.

"Oh my God," I mumbled. "Oh, fuck." I let the hose play through my hands as it uncoiled, ready to pull Marco out as soon as twenty seconds had elapsed. I counted as fast as I could: "One-Mississippi-two-Mississippi-three-Mississippi—"

The hose began to slip through my fingers faster . . . and faster . . . and faster. My skin burned from the friction of the rubber zipping across my palms. It seemed impossible that the puddle could be deep enough to consume dozens of feet of hose, but it was.

"Marco!" I tried to close my hands around the hose, but I was almost jerked off my feet by the force of whatever was pulling it. I had to let it go or risk getting yanked into the puddle myself. Just as the final coils of the hose unfolded, whatever had grabbed it—*had grabbed Marco*—stopped. I tentatively gripped the hose and hauled it hand-over-hand out of the water. It came out easily. Too easily. After about a dozen feet, the end emerged. It was cleanly severed.

"Marco?" My voice was barely a whisper. The tears in my eyes spilled over. The hose slipped from my fingers and fell to the ground. The severed end flopped into the puddle. There was no splash.

A quick flash of movement in the water made my heart trip in my chest. I felt a swell of hope at the possibility that my friends were surfacing from the depths . . . followed by a surge of unspeakable horror at what I saw instead. It was something so alien, so incomprehensible, so *other* that I struggle to describe it in terms anyone can understand. It reminded me of the hind leg of a grasshopper—long, skinny, barbed, jointed—but twice as long as my arm and made of something that looked like black glass. At the end was a churning cluster of smaller appendages that moved like the mouthparts of a crab. They had the ghostly translucency of white quartz crystals, but they were as dexterous and multi-jointed as my own fingers.

The nightmare limb breached the surface of the puddle and extended in my direction. I stumbled backward, tripping over my own feet and falling on my back. Two more identical limbs emerged beside the first. They pressed into the ground by my feet as the creature began to lift itself out of the puddle. With a desperate cry, I drove my heels into the dirt, propelling myself away from the water as fast as I could. Then I rolled over, scrambled to my feet, and ran.

I ran past Eddie's house, down Grape Street, and all the way to my house on Peachtree Lane. Throwing the front door open, I sprinted across the kitchen to the phone on the wall and dialed 911. The operator thought I was making a crank call, but after a few minutes of pleading, I was able to convince her to send the Rescue Squad to Eddie's house. Then I hung up the phone and ran back the way I came. By the time I got to the lot, sweat-soaked and gasping for breath, the police were already there.

But the puddle was gone.

All that was left in the lot were Eddie's sneakers, socks, and t-shirt, exactly where he had tossed them. There was no sign of Eddie, Shah, or Marco. Just like the puddle, they had vanished.

I explained to the police exactly what happened, but they didn't believe me. How could they? A disappearing puddle? Water that doesn't splash? A trio of giant grasshopper legs with alien finger-mouths? I sounded like an insane person who had rented too many horror movies from West Coast Video.

Instead, the police had a much more realistic theory: the boys had run away from home. They assumed I was covering for them—albeit badly—by concocting a crazy story to account for their disappearance. The cops could never explain *why* the boys might have run away or where they might have run away to, but it didn't matter. For the next twenty years, that was the official explanation. It's what Shah's parents believed when they moved back to India, what Marco's mom believed when she hung herself in the garage the next summer, and what Eddie's parents believed when they died in their sleep from carbon monoxide poisoning a few months ago.

After Eddie's folks were gone, a wealthy investor bought their land and knocked down their house so he could build a new mini-mansion on the property. With the addition of the empty lot next door, the new owner had enough room to add a tennis court, a putting green, and even an in-ground pool. It was during the excavation of the pool that a new clue to my friends' whereabouts was found. The construction workers hadn't dug up any bodies or bones, or anything gruesome like that. But a dozen feet underground, in the exact spot where the puddle had been, they made an unexpected find: a large cave with a puddle of strange, silvery liquid inside. And, beside the puddle?

An old Wiffle ball.

A yellow plastic bat.

And a tangle of rotten garden hose.

Some of the cops who had investigated my friends' disappearance were still on the force, so they immediately recognized the significance of the discovery. They contacted me and implored me to drive the four hours from my apartment in Pennsylvania so they could question me once again about what had transpired that day.

I decided to crash at my parents' house on Peachtree Lane while the police conducted their investigation. My dad had passed away a few years earlier, but his commendations were still proudly displayed in a case on the mantel, along with the famous photo of him shaking hands with Nixon after receiving his Medal of Honor. There was also a plaque with his favorite quote engraved on it, from Shakespeare's *Julius Caesar*: "Cowards die many times before their deaths; The valiant never taste of death but once."

There was no question that my dad had died once and only once. But me, on the other hand? I had tried following in my dad's footsteps by joining the Army after high school, but I couldn't even make it through basic training. The closest I ever got to a Medal of Honor was winning the Saturday night darts championship at my local bar. And I was still afraid of the dark. I was the coward Caesar warned about, dying again and again every time I let my fear stop me from doing the right thing.

The police forensics teams spent the better part of a week poking through the dirt and clay for any other evidence that might provide a clue to my friends' whereabouts, but in the end, they found nothing. They closed the case again and told me I was free to go. But I didn't. Instead, I drove my rental car to the empty lot where my friends had disappeared.

With the investigation complete and with construction yet to resume, it was easy for me to access the lot without anyone noticing. I ducked under the police tape, then slid down the steep side of the muddy hole to the entrance of the cave where the bat, ball, and hose had been found. It was a low, flat space, maybe twenty feet across, with a domed ceiling striped with sedimentary rock. The excavation had collapsed one side of the cave, turning it into rubble and exposing it to the open air. Even in the dark, the puddle inside was just as shiny and strange as I remembered.

As I stared at the water, I thought about what happened that day, about how the lot which had been such a source of joy for us had turned into such a nightmare. I thought about Joe Montana and Jerry Rice, about Mark McGwire and Jose Canseco, about Terminator and RoboCop. I thought about Marco, and Eddie, and Shah. I thought about my father. If I had been more like my dad, maybe my friends would have still been alive. Not a day went by where I didn't wish I had gone into the water after them. Maybe I couldn't have saved them, but at least I wouldn't have had to live with the fact that I didn't even try.

After a few minutes of standing in silence, I sat down on the rubble at the edge of the puddle and took off my sneakers. I removed my shirt and pants, folded them neatly on the ground, then placed my shoes on top, along with my wallet, car keys, and flip phone. Then I closed my eyes, held my breath, and stepped into the water. It was warm, so warm that it barely registered as being wet. It felt comforting, almost womb-like. It surrounded me, cradled me, embraced me. As I allowed myself to sink into the Stygian abyss, I felt calm. Peaceful. Content.

Then, something grabbed my leg.

I should have been scared. I should have been terrified. But I wasn't.

For the first time in my life, I didn't feel any fear at all.

A Plain, Ordinary Woman

~ Jennifer Worrell

Never use a dull razor to get the job done.

Desima smoothed hot oil over her naked, brown self, ensuring every hair had been waxed, shaved, or zapped from existence. Besides eyebrows and lashes, only her crimson-tipped faux-hawk remained as the barest obligatory effort toward meeting beauty standards. Other girls could keep the waves that undulated to the floor, the boldly colored tresses fanned into exotic flowers, the braids engineered into architectural marvels.

Sweeping the pad of her thumb under her chin, she huffed at a bristly patch that she missed. Desima angled her face to catch the light and stretched her skin over her jaw. The whisker emerged hazy black just beneath the surface. She relit her body oil candle and poked the tip of a cuticle scissor in until it glowed. Snagging the blade under the hair, she met a gentle resistance but scraped it free. She flicked her finger over the tip, a delicious quiver vibrating along her neck. She grabbed the tweezers and yanked hard enough to savor the rip. A fat root glistened like a ripe plum. A rush of calm filled her head, like the roar of the sea inside a conch. One less imperfection, one less beacon drawing attention. The hours spent on this ritual, the constant tenderness that followed, was worth it for a week of invisibility, wolven blood be damned.

She clicked off the high-beam fluorescent bulb and stored her beauty kit in a drawer, slamming it harder than she intended. Idiot boys and outdated traditions—encouraging randos to stroke the tresses of their objects of desire like some creepy valentine—tended to cause that reaction. Too bad her school didn't spend a week before the annual Wolf Moon Festival teaching unpaired students how to mind one's own business instead of new coiffing techniques. But all this pageantry, the styling competitions, the inexplicit yet shamefully direct theme of mating, deepened the connection to their lupine ancestors, who were more inclined to re-inhabit their human progeny during this time of year more than any other, or so the logic went. Another event that managed to both dismiss and spotlight women like her.

A sour taste flooded Desima's mouth. She wished she were outside childbearing age, the only group sheltered against such nonsense. Until those years were over, she'd be surrounded by boys blowing on the nape of her neck and sighing at the baby hairs waving back at them, licking their lips whenever she kicked off her shoes, hoping to glimpse a dark line leading from toe to ankle. Every summer she contemplated never going barefoot again, wearing long sleeves and pants to cover her limbs, maybe even shaving her scalp as bare as the rest of her.

But covering up made it worse; their imaginations ran wild, speculating what treasures lay underneath, hardly able to keep their hands to themselves.

Centuries after their lineage was diluted to merely distant kin, too many boys still acted like animals, their memories failing to remember all the yesterdays when she recoiled at the slightest touch from anyone outside her small platonic circle, wanting simply to inhabit her own space and air.

Counting to ten, massaging her jaw in tiny circles, Desima reminded herself to breathe. Stress mercifully made some people bald, but cursed her in the opposite direction. She steeled herself for another day at Lupine High, followed by a two-hour-long Festival Committee meeting, mandatory for seniors.

At least she could console herself with the fact that everyone else wanted to sit in the glare of floodlights, both literally and figuratively—on stage at the history re-enactment, hawking wares at the vendor booths, guiding children's story circles—leaving her alone with the job of prop master. Except for Peter, who she volunteered as her assistant. If she had to suffer through this, she was roping her best friend in too. And since this was his first year in the village, the grandeur of her heritage was yet unspoiled by exploitation, the mystique surrounding the old tales still ripe with wonder. Despite the bastardization of history into a commercial spectacle, some magic remained in it all.

☉

Staring blankly into the turd-brown void in the back of her locker, mind swimming with pre-meeting contingency plans and inventories and all things werewolf, Desima momentarily let her guard down. Before registering the swell of derisive laughter, she sensed a rank change in the air. From the corner of her eye, she saw Uri and his band of Neanderthals slither into a half-circle behind her, preventing easy escape.

"Imagine how pretty she'd be if she grew that hair out."

Desima groped along a row of hooks in the side wall of the locker for her set of knuckle spikes. Shaped like two innocent puppies curled up together, her fingers fit snugly through the eyeholes, ears stabbing between. With her free hand, she pulled a notebook with a silvery cover off the top shelf. The shiny object would distract the boys long enough to conceal the weapon in her pocket.

She turned to see fat fingers, lined with dirt and stinking of piss, hovering inches from her face.

"What the fuck?" Desima knocked John's hand away with the notebook but the dull slap echoing down the hall only made them laugh.

"Almost got a handful, guys." John's sniveling voice was enough to make her fantasize about raking those cute little ears across his jugular.

"What do you want, I'm late for Festival Committee."

They crept closer, their eyes glazed, transfixed on Desima's faux-hawk. "We just want to touch it," John said. "What is it with you?"

Her skin pricked as if she had a legit allergy to them. She itched to roll down her sleeves but they'd pounce on any vulnerability. Shouting for help would probably bring the wrong teacher running, one who'd find this all very charming.

Desima flashed to sixth grade, at a memory she thought had disappeared. Uri and some friend of his had shoved her against the schoolyard fence at recess, balled the top of her t-shirt in his fist, and stared inside, inspecting her sternum for the first fine curls. They tossed her aside, bored, when they saw she was still bare. She'd looked up to see the recess monitors watching like this assault was no big deal, her worth linked exclusively to her physique.

That night she bought her guard dogs and painted the tips with ox blood, then chopped off her knee-length mane and buried the scraps. Once the novelty of her new cut wore off, no one gave her a second glance, and she'd never needed to use the blades. But the Wolf Moon Festival tended to bring out the beast in people.

The boys' arms dangled as they swayed on the balls of their feet. The hall vanished behind their hulking bodies.

Stifling a yawn, she blinked slowly and set her face to stone.

"Give us a little something." This one had a pretentious name like Zacc. He wore a shirt with a v-neck so exaggerated it exposed his bushy chest and abs, coming to a point at the waist of his pants.

Desima averted her eyes and gnashed her teeth to keep her last meal down.

Zacc raked his fingers over his bushy pecs, a mist of sweat glistening in the fluorescent light. "Maybe I can feel yours against mine." He snatched at her blouse with a hooked finger.

She let her notebook clatter to the floor.

"Relax, honey." Uri licked his wet, gaping mouth.

"I'm not your fucking honey." The air whistled as she drew her claws in an arc.

The boys sprang back, shock replacing lust and intrigue on their faces. Except Uri, who broadened his chest, calling her bluff. A tough-girl façade made from paper and paint.

So predictable.

She swung again, so close his thin shirt billowed. He screwed up his mouth and snatched at the weapon, but she struck like a rattlesnake, piercing his palm. As he pressed the heel of his other hand into the wound, she turned her wrist and jabbed his bicep.

Desima grinned at his yelp of pain and John and Zacc retreating down the adjoining hall.

"You bitch," Uri said, pulling the pencil out of his bun to twist his sleeve into a tourniquet. "You won't have those with you all the time, so—"

Desima stared him dead in the eye, unblinking, and licked his blood off the blades. He turned a unique shade of white and took off after his friends.

The muscles in her arms rippled as though trying to shake off a layer of filthy water. She rolled her shoulders and neck but the feeling wouldn't leave. Uri's voice spread inside her mind. She shuddered at the idea of John's scaly fingers finding their mark, tugging the wiry tip of a curl.

Her body tingled like a rash. She thrust her hands under her sleeves to scratch. A thatch of peach fuzz lined her upper arms. She could see it, faintly, through the white cotton. Most likely the boys could too. They could smell the sweat clinging to every strand, the scent of panic and fury a special kind of perfume.

The day of the festival, Desima was up an hour early, trying to decide between her regular, everyday hoodie or her special occasion hoodie, excited to finally get this mess over with. By nightfall, the rust-red moon hung close enough to touch. The naked branches of the trees had turned to crystal. An inch of snow covered the ground, sparkling with a frosty glaze.

As if superstitious, the planners kept everything the same, down to the food and the paper lanterns lining the arcade. Bright lights and cloying vapors poured from the competitors' ring, where tournaments for most impressive styling drew white-knuckled spectators. Sultry music snaked beneath a purple voile curtain, giving visitors a glimpse of ladies in skimpy outfits performing burlesque dances by torchflame.

Outside noise dulled to a mellow drone as Desima stalked through the dim light of the prop tent, checking inventory against her clipboard. A mirrored dressing table filled with scraps of fabric and sewing notions, random make-up jars and first-aid supplies, sat lopsided among wood trunks and boxes. A mat of straw lined soil still damp from snow and ice. The wolf costume hung centered against one wall, isolated by velvet ropes and accented by spotlights.

Every year the re-enactment required a new costume, and every year the head seemed larger, the mouth crowded with dagger-like fangs. The fibers of the eyes were painted by hand with a single hair from a wolf's tail. Desima leaned in, losing herself in the inky pools of crimson at the center. The pelt's reddish tint implied the hunter returning from a kill, perhaps prowling for another, its belly never sated. The scent was as real as the rest of it: canine mixed with rust and meat, sulfur and smoke.

A surprisingly loud growl tore through her stomach. Though she ate before her shift, planning to score her much-earned free plates of barbecue once the masses started heading home, she didn't know if she could wait that long. According to her watch, there was no time for a break. She ignored the scent of roasted meat wafting through the flaps in the tent and busied herself searching for broken stitches, loose teeth and hair, anything that might come undone on stage. Nothing ruins an atmosphere more than the main attraction falling apart.

After double-stitching a couple of trouble spots, she stepped back to admire her handiwork. A strange flutter curled around her heart. Each artist brought distinct interpretations to their work, trying to make their re-creations of the ancestral beast more realistic, more unsettling, than the last. They always fell short of the mark. This year they outdid themselves, though she couldn't quite articulate why. Something about the depth of the eyes brought a chill of familiarity.

"Deeeesima." Uri's voice wormed through the tent. "Desimaaa."

Nothing in the tent was substantial enough to hide behind. John and Zacc might be waiting outside to trap her if she ran.

For once Desima wished Peter was at her elbow. Though his small stature and quiet voice made him an easy target for bullies, they usually threw a few taunts and otherwise left him alone. A guy who posed no threat in terms of brawn tended to be nearly as invisible as a sexually indifferent woman. They'd probably move along before risking rejection in front of a guy outside their pack.

She ducked under the pelt, careful not to dislodge it from the hooks that held it aloft. The fur felt soft, intimate. The front paws dangled low enough to conceal her dusty gray shoes, and the spotlights threw imposing, disorienting shadows.

Rusty iron stakes held the velvet ropes in place. She contemplated pulling one out for protection, cursing herself for leaving her guard dogs at home. Believing she was safe with the entire village milling around now seemed infinitely stupid. She nudged a stake in the rear with her toe and it wiggled.

Through small mesh-covered eyeholes over the snout, she saw three silhouettes lumbering through the front of the tent. She tugged at the stake, ignoring the pain of the jagged edges perforating her skin. Sweat greased her palms, fingernails squealing against metal as her grip slipped upward. Gritting her teeth, she strangled the stake and pulled, holding her breath even as it burned for release. They would not find her here, would not fucking touch one inch of her body, even if it meant dislocating her shoulders. Finally the stake eased from the earth.

As they neared her hiding place, they lowered their voices and stepped as delicately as ballet dancers on glass. Zacc tilted his head and paused. They seemed to be eye to eye.

Desima tensed, hefting the stake. It was heavy. Too heavy to swing with any efficiency.

Zacc lunged forward, but was knocked nearly off his feet.

"The fuck are you doing?" Uri moved into view, squaring his shoulders.

"What—"

"Get away from that." Uri's voice wavered as though he feared the costume would come to life. "What if it falls in the *dirt*?"

"Sorry man, whatever."

"Not *whatever*. Watch it."

"Hey," John called, from the rear of the tent. How did Desima not see him pass by? Who else did she miss? "She's probably backstage. Let's get out of here before we mess something up."

The crunch of straw slowly diminished, but the threat of an unmet challenge emerged in their wake.

Desima extracted herself from the costume, dropping the stake. She scratched her brow, itchy from the hot fur, but her fingers ignited in pain. A wet trail remained, too sticky to be sweat. She stepped in front of the battered dressing table and inspected herself in the cracked mirror. Blood covered the tips of her fingers where her nails had popped off, leaving gory little stumps.

She cleaned herself up with sterile wipes and wrapped her fingertips in bandages, then readjusted her hood and slipped on a pair of fingerless gloves. She'd sent Peter to the stage with a box full of last-minute decorations, so she figured she'd hunt him down to make sure he was okay. Hopefully Uri and his gang got sidetracked and stayed out of Peter's way.

Outside, volunteers weaved among passersby with samples of sweets and spiced nuts. Musicians roamed the crowd, keeping the spirit lively and joyous, encouraging people to pair off into folk dances.

Some of the couples huddled around stalls for snacks and beer or an excuse to catch their breath between songs. Desima snorted at the men in curly-haired chaps and matching vests emulating fauns. Many of the women wore mittens like wolves' paws or fur leg warmers under short skirts.

Things hadn't changed much since grade school parties, where all girls talked about was boys and how to snag one, from sundown until moonrise, when they traded strategies for dreams.

Coals from fire pits turned icicles clinging to the fringed canopies into twinkling fairy lights. Though the arcade was warmly lit, the staging area between it and the woods fell into shadow. Desima dodged the throng and weaved among mazes of power cords and generators and ice chests, the boring stuff no one gave a second thought to. Between her all-gray clothes and scruffy shoes worn silent, she melted into the background like another set piece.

Treading the boundary between civilization and wilderness, a crackling, guttural noise resonated deep within the trees. Something lingered, hungry. The shadows moved with the wind, a swell of forest out of sync with reality.

She stayed rooted to her spot. The air hummed with tension. The sound of claws digging in the hard-packed ground seemed inches away, but she could see nothing past the dark cloud obscuring the parcel of trees directly ahead. A pair of crimson lights burned into her retinas. The sensation felt like fire in the hearth.

"Des."

She blinked and the red lights receded, the impenetrable blackness blown away. An owl swooped from its pine-bough sanctuary.

Desima turned toward the arcade and a pair of distinctively out-of-style pants carrying their owner into view. "Peter?"

"What are you doing hanging out in the dark like some Goth?"

The lanterns gave Peter a halo effect, highlighting a peach balayage pompadour with an undercut resembling tiger stripes. So that's where he'd been all this time. He must have booked a spot well in advance.

"Bored already?"

"This is *incredible*. You sold it way short."

"I see you got your hair designed."

Peter nodded crisply, then froze, softly touching the waves to make sure they didn't bounce out of place. "So is the front row reserved for staff? Do we get to skip the line or—"

"Chill. Show's not for . . ." Desima checked her watch. Five minutes. How long had she been staring into the woods? "Don't worry, we're getting bird's-eye seats. Follow me."

Desima led Peter through the performers' entrance of the pavilion and up the scaffolding. Sidling past the lighting tech, she perched on the edge of the catwalk hovering above the stage. Peter scootched in close. Any other boy even suggesting this would make her body stiffen and angle toward the exit to regain even an inch of space, but Peter's disinterest matched her own.

The conductor rapped his music stand and the audience's excitement hushed. The house lights dimmed and sweeping symphonic music drowned out the last tittering voices. As the music faded, the narrator's rich baritone thundered into the pavilion and pulsed in Desima's chest.

"Many centuries ago, wolf and human were inseparable. They formed alliances, eventually resulting in offspring, and the first true werewolf was born."

Dawn gleamed over the rocky landscape. Spears and slings were symbolically tucked stage right as man and wolf enjoyed the heat of a fire side by side.

Traditionally, the play was done almost entirely in pantomime, allowing actors to add personal touches that made it worth watching time and again, while the audience's imaginations and familial histories filled in what dialogue left out.

The second act was immersed in war and struggle, the waning sun mutating to blood red, mountains and fallow fields falling into grim twilight.

"Centuries of ecological and political strife, plague and famine, took their toll, causing both beast and man to lose touch with their roots and separate."

The land appeared ravaged, the result of scrabbling hands searching for bulbs and roots as well as a place to bury the many dead. The wolf at center stage seemed immense, powerful enough to bound into the rafters.

"Despite the broken bonds of the past, each being kept aspects of the other's essence."

The exit music swelled as the red backlighting morphed to the golden warmth of optimism and endurance.

Desima held her gaze on the scene, captivated by the crystal glint in the wolf's eyes. Her mouth echoed the coda as if summoned.

"People believe during Wolf Moons, they can transform from human to wolf and vice versa."

"Do you believe that too?"

Desima needed a second to readjust to reality. She nearly forgot Peter was there. The house lights came up as the curtain descended, widening the divide for another year.

"First time for everything." *And damn, would it be nice.* Reluctantly she stood, swatting Peter's shoulder. "Come on. Let's go grab the costume before it gets trampled."

After picking up the specially molded crate from the prop tent, nestling the costume and head inside, and returning it to a safe corner, Desima snuck out to nab a few kabobs and ciders to toast their hard work. One of the vendors even slipped her chunks of shortcake. She and Peter perched on trunks and dawdled through their late-night snack, lost in their own thoughts. As he stretched across the domed lid and licked his fingers clean, Desima gave one last look around.

"All right, there goes your first Wolf Moon Festival, friend."

"We're done already?"

"Yep. The historical society comes for the costume, and porters take down the tents and stuff. We're out."

Peter flicked off the lights and they headed toward the woods, navigating around the heavily rutted ground. He flinched at a howling sound.

"Just the wind," Desima assured him. "How 'bout I walk you home?"

"You don't have to." He didn't sound convincing.

"It's on the way."

The fairgrounds were deserted except for the last few vendors packing up their trucks. Some of the arcade lanterns remained lit, but without anyone operating the stalls, they cast a sinister glow. The wind whipped up, making trees shiver and banners crackle and snap.

"Anyway, I need to protect you from ghosts," Desima said, running her fingers up Peter's arm.

"Ghost footsteps are awfully loud," he muttered, looking suspiciously over his shoulder.

Desima chuckled, but perked up her ears. A third patter of steps joined theirs, then a fourth. The fifth couldn't be far behind.

She grabbed Peter's hand and picked up the pace. But even the most normal movements feel awkward when someone's watching. Her knees jutted out like a scarecrow's. Her jeans seemed to fit wrong, shifting around her legs with each step.

Locking his sights on the edge of the tree line, Peter tripped over a root. Or a cable. Or—

"Figured you were still creeping around." Uri grabbed Desima by the shoulder and forced her to face him. Zacc crouched closer, holding something she couldn't make out.

Peter tried to scramble to his feet, but John stepped on his foot to hold him down. His stance was sloppy, unsteady, like he'd never been in a fight and was unprepared for this one. In the tent earlier, his voice betrayed the same weakness. She hoped she read him correctly.

Uri shoved her back, swinging his foot out to topple her balance. The seam of her jeans ripped as she landed. Pressing her palms into the dirt, she kicked at Uri's groin, but he tilted his hips. She sprang up on her heels, turning to help Peter up, but froze at the snick of a switchblade.

A knife glinted against Zacc's thigh.

Uri's bicep jumped with the flick of his lever. "Told you we'd catch you without your blades."

Desima backed up slowly toward Peter. John laughed as he forced his weight down. Peter yelped and punched the kid's knees. John wobbled, and Desima caught a pearly shimmer in his right pocket. He had a blade too, and either didn't know how to use it or didn't want to.

"Peter, you got this?" Desima caught his eye and tapped her hip.

He bit his lip and stared at her so long she wasn't sure he understood. Then he grabbed the toe of John's shoe with one hand and twisted the heel in the opposite direction. John fell on top of Peter, knocking the wind out of them both. As the two boys wrestled in the snow, Desima grabbed the edge of John's pocket and yanked, howling at the pain in her shredded fingers. The bandages wormed away from her skin, and new nails, straight-tipped and sharp as razors, sheared through the latex.

The knife slid from the torn denim, landing in a circle of snow and bloody bandages. She pressed the button with her left hand and poked it awkwardly into John's side. He didn't need much persuasion to move. Rather than trying to help his friends or reclaim his knife, he ran off into the woods, skidding on patches of ice. Desima would have laughed if her fingers didn't feel like they were being split open from the inside.

Peter held up his fists, but his boxing expertise came from movies and old TV shows. Zacc saw his opportunity and slashed Peter's pristine white shirt. He sucked in his belly and readjusted his stance, fist colliding with Zacc's cheek. Desima waved John's switch in Uri's face, but he thrust at her stomach, driving her further into the trees. Wind gusted through the hole in her sweatshirt. She didn't dare look down, but considering the chill, the gash must have been six inches long.

Her right hand felt shredded, but at the same time swollen and numb. Uri lunged again, plunging the knife into her shoulder.

She shouted for Peter but was sure the sound of tearing flesh drowned her out. Her entire body seemed to inflate, engorged and ready to explode.

Desima tipped her head into the snow. When had she fallen? The intense cold was a welcome sensation, blocking the pain and distended sensation of her limbs.

Uri kneeled on her hip and held the knife at her throat. Desima noticed a male figure running at them, but it was Zacc. Where the hell was Peter?

"Took you long enough," Uri snapped.

"I had something to get rid of," Zacc said, shaking droplets from his knife. Blood dotted the snow at his feet.

"Peter!"

Uri and Zacc ignored her as they shredded her jeans and her sleeves and widened the hole in her sweatshirt, careful to pull the cloth away from her skin.

They drew back, gasping in awe. Sweat poured off her stomach in streams, soaking the fabric, hair sticking to her body. She reached up to her chin, now covered in soft fuzz.

They panted, fascinated, twirling individual strands between their fingers, leaning down to sniff and nuzzle, a contented thrum rising between them. They left her underwear alone, her breasts unmolested, like some perverted sign of respect.

Desima clamped her jaw shut, incisors stabbing into her bottom lip. Breathing hard through her nose, another heaving voice answered her own.

She tensed her hands, surprised her fingers no longer hurt. The stumps of her fingers had been replaced by rigid black claws, casting skeletal shadows in the snow.

Uri pulled off her shoes and socks and tossed them aside. He delicately raised her ankles, inspecting her like rare gemstones, when his eyes went wide at the sight of two massive paws where human feet used to be.

"What the *fuck* . . ."

She kicked up, snapping out of his grip. A delicious crunch caused Zacc to whip his head up. Desima raked her forepaws across his face, stripping his nose to ribbons. He screamed and covered his face, but not before a waterfall of blood gushed into his lap.

Uri was too stunned to make a sound. He snuffled through his broken septum and writhed backwards on his hands, but Desima clamped her fangs into his calf, siphoning warm blood and flesh between her teeth. The boys' screams rang thin and high as they squeezed air from their lungs.

She'd heard a similar sound, halfway in and out of sleep, at some long-ago slumber party. Instead of frightened, Desima had been fascinated, partial witness to terrors only her friend could see.

Uri's face distorted with astonishment and rage. Zacc tackled Uri before he could do anything stupid.

Desima rose up on her hind legs, snarling, barely conscious of the figure beside her.

Peter bent, clutching at his middle, to pick up one of the fallen switchblades. Before anyone had time to react, he jerked forward, impaling Zacc's wrist.

Zacc shrieked, lurching into the woods with Uri stumbling behind.

Desima's fingers uncurled, slowly shrinking to their original form. Her limbs, still thick with muscle, ached with the fresh buzz of a morning stretch.

"You okay, Peter?"

Peter sliced off his sleeves and knotted them into a pressure bandage across his skinny waist. A purple ring blossomed around one eye and a corner of his mouth.

"Yeah . . . he didn't cut me so deep after all, I guess. You, though—" Peter tilted his head, his expression a mixture of bemusement and delight.

Desima caught sight of herself in a frozen puddle, her hair disintegrating, muzzle and fangs retracting with a soft crackling static. Her bones snugged into her flesh with an easy tightness, like stepping from a hot bath into the chill of an open window.

"Never better."

Peter sheared off her own tattered sleeve and knotted it over her shoulder, which was already beginning to heal.

Desima could still hear the boys' keening in the distance. She considered whether she'd ever be haunted by that sound, or if it would come back to her on a future moonlit January, carried on the crisp air like a symphony.

Nine Times

~ K. Wallace King

I

The moon is a horned crescent pressed against the sky. Duncan snores softly on the pillow beside her and she turns her head to his profile. He is outlined in moonlight, still as a marble effigy. He could be dead lying there beside her. The cat twitches, its purr vibrates her palm when she strokes it. It's so hot. Suffocating. The air conditioner must have shut itself off. The air stinks from the herbs in the candle; cinnamon, myrrh, aloe. Molly fell asleep with it burning. She bought the candle at a quirky shop—clever greeting cards, tee-shirts with silkscreened pentacles—hipster sorcery. She had picked up a book, *Witch Bitch/Reclaiming Our Fire*. A gift for Cattie's birthday? Cattie played at being a witch. Cattie was her best friend. Most of the time. Some of the time. Not much anymore. Actually, Molly couldn't remember the last time she'd seen Cattie. She'd put the book back, but purchased the candle. It was black and had a label she couldn't read because she didn't have her glasses.

"They used these herbs for wrapping mummies," said the girl in The Sisters of Mercy tee shirt as she put the candle in a bag.

In Molly's bedroom the melted wax and burnt herbs make her feel ill.

II

A half full glass of red wine glows in the lunar light. Molly sits up and the sheet slips to the floor in a puddle. Her heart slips too. Duncan isn't here and he's never coming back. "I can't get close to you." That's what he'd said as he packed his things. "You've got your weapon drawn to cut anyone near your heart."

Molly takes a gulp of the wine, grimacing at the sour vinegar of it after sitting in the heat. As she swallows the rest of the wine, a mouse, its tail twitching, quivers on the floor beside her bed. *Just a trick of the light*, thinks Molly, as she kicks the old catnip toy out of sight.

The cat died. The vet told her that the jerky spasms were only muscles responding to the drug, that it was painless, but Molly didn't believe him. She was to blame for this bad death. The cat had cancer, but she'd refused to let it go. When it cried Molly had shushed it, stroking the dull fur, "It's alright. One more day." Without the cat she would be all alone. With herself.

As it was dying, the vet placed the cat in her arms. Molly had shoved it back to the veterinarian. "I can't. I can't." She had rushed away, leaving the cat she'd had for fourteen years to die with a stranger.

Molly picks up her phone from the bedside table. It's only midnight. She puts a hand to her crashing heart. She looks out the window and sees the moon is not a crescent. It is fat and full, hanging heavy over the hills. The cratered face is so visible Molly's eyes might be telescopes.

Moonlight spotlights the driveway as a coyote, thin and ragged, trots across, carrying something in its mouth. The coyote pauses and, as if it knows Molly is watching, lifts its head to the window. The thing in its mouth wriggles helplessly. From somewhere across the canyon Molly thinks she hears a woman screaming.

III

There's a witch moon through the window and the hills are humps of shadow. A sound grates in her mind, a picture forms. A woman, dark haired, in a diaphanous gown drags a steel sword behind her as she walks down a sidewalk. It grates like a rasping scream. She thinks it will drive her crazy, like the houses that tower over her, leering with windowed eyes, with open-doored mouths. Duncan is dim, distant, on a rocky shore while Molly is aboard a pitching rowboat in wild water, a serpentine river—she watches the coils of it unwind before her.

Angry water slaps the boat, oars dangle like lifeless limbs in the river, and Molly is trying to cry out for help but her throat, how it burns. Where did Duncan go? There he is. Standing against a purpling sky with a hook for the moon. He is but a shadow, a wavering shade on the shore.

Black smoke rises, obscuring Duncan. Like a tornado touching down, the cloud of smoke extends what looks like a leg, then another, until there are four. Molly watches the billowing smoke churn and swirl until the smear of black looks remarkably like a great soot-footed dog.

"Row," says someone behind her. "Row, row." Molly turns, clutching the sides of the bucking rowboat, but she is alone. Red lights flash on the shoreline. The boat rocks dangerously, almost throwing her into the river. Approaching sirens shrill like a woman screaming.

IV

The moon is a lopsided egg hanging above the hills. Duncan snores softly on the pillow beside her, she can just make out his profile. The cat mews piteously, she feels the purr vibrate when she strokes it. A dove laments in the loquat tree outside the window. Or is it an owl? Owls eat smaller birds, gentler birds, they tear their insides out. *Horrible.* She doesn't want this thought in her head as she closes her eyes. *Sunflowers.* She grows a garden of big bright flowers, their shining faces—

Duncan says, "Row."

"Honey." Molly gently pokes Duncan's shoulder. "You're talking in your sleep."

"Row."

Even though he is on the pillow beside her, he sounds far way. *What did you say?* Molly tries to turn her face to Duncan beside her on the bed because this is a dream, this boat, the blurred black dog, but she cannot move. She is paralyzed. Yet Molly feels her heart madly fluttering, terrified feathers batting against bone.

OH wake up wake up wake up.

Molly opens her eyes and witnesses her hands flapping wildly above her body. They shine pale as dove wings in the light of the moon. *Thank god it was only—I was dreaming.* She drops her hands. Beside her the cat still purrs. She snuggles up against Duncan, lays her head on his chest, inhaling the sleepy fragrance of his skin. "Are you awake? Oh Jesus, Duncan. I was having the weirdest dream. Duncan? No answer. Molly once more opens her eyes. Outside the window the moon is laughing.

She pulls down the shade and turns on the bedside lamp. She reads mindless garbage then plays games on her phone until it says it's morning. When she tugs the bottom of the window shade, it curls around the roller at the top with the sound of a slap. The room smells of greasy smoke, burnt herbs.

V

Molly takes her coffee to the balcony and sits there in her tee shirt and underwear. She watches the full moon fade as the sun rises, turning the sky a wounded pink before spreading into a vast dome of metallic blue. She can already feel the heat trapped in the wood of the boards beneath her feet. It is another day of temperatures over ninety-five, even though it is late October. Molly watches two crows surfing the updraft over the houses clumped on the the hillsides above the canyon. She thinks about what she might do today, but nothing comes to mind. Another day of in-between. Between jobs, between relationships, pets. *Hell, my life.*

Molly leans on the railing of the balcony. She had once been able to see the entire Hollywood sign. It was the reason she'd agreed to pay more than she could comfortably afford for the apartment. That had been eleven, no, twelve years ago. *How could I have let it all slip by?* Now trees on the hillside have grown much taller and new houses have been built. The famous sign is obscured except for the *H*, one *O*, a solitary *L*, and the *W*. Molly rearranges the letters in her mind. If she could howl maybe she wouldn't feel so empty. But the neighbors would hear. She feels she is turning into that woman that neighbors whisper about behind her back. She'd once known many of the people on her street, but the familiar faces have disappeared.

When a breeze stirs, Molly smells smoke from the fire blazing north off the 5 freeway. Fire is a season in California. The hills are the beige of dead vegetation. The crows call to one another as they circle. In the sunlit sky, their black wings outspread, they dive like bats. Their shrieks make Molly think of the grate of metal. What should she do today? Every day feels the same. Molly looks up. The birds are gone. Not a single cloud. The sky is empty. *Like me.*

☉

VI

On the street below the balcony a woman is pulling something out of her dog's mouth. She recognizes the woman as a neighbor. Molly waves, but the woman doesn't see her and tosses whatever the dog had in its mouth into the bushes as they walk away. Molly decides to take a walk herself. It's something to do and if she waits any longer it will be too hot to move.

A half hour later she's sweating. She has neglected to bring a hat and regrets it. The sun is blistering. She has climbed the winding streets above her apartment building and finds herself farther up in the hills than she'd intended. She can't remember what kept her so preoccupied that she hadn't noticed. She must have been thinking deeply to not have even seen the mob of tourists around Lake Hollywood, she doesn't even recall hiking past it.

It's easy to get lost in the Hollywood hills. Streets begin at one point and snake upward, sometimes concluding in a surprising dead end. Or, you'll drive into the hills and, before you know it, find yourself descending into the San Fernando valley with no idea how you got there or how to return to where you started.

Molly is panting as she climbs the steep street. She passes houses perched precariously on the hillside, greedy for every available foot, every inch of coveted view. The architecture she passes is a jarring jangle of periods and styles. A seventies-era geodesic dome with mirror-tinted windows is wedged between a Spanish revival and a

Disneyesque McMansion with fairy tale turrets. As she passes a mock Tudor an unseen dog begins to bay. The woeful sound trails behind her. Something flashes in the dirt beside the pavement. A coin. She turns it over in her palm. It is copper-colored, like a penny, but much larger. It must be foreign, she doesn't recognize the faded images. *Big enough to cover an eye.* Why did she think that? Shuddering, she flings the coin into a bush and resumes her hike.

She pauses, smelling smoke more strongly and scans the sky. It's still cloudless, the one-note turquoise of a dyed Easter egg. A memory tugs—Molly in a candy-pink dress. A little woven basket. The other kids faces are smeared with chocolate rabbits.

"Don't just stand there," says her father with a little shove, "join the hunt."

But when the grownups retreat inside, Molly is the hunted. The children run her down across the green lawn, through the rotating sprinklers. She slips and falls onto the lawn, smearing her dress bowel brown in the damp dirt. She lies there, frozen as marble, when the howling children surround her. Then the boy, brown-eyed, black haired, the one she liked, dumps the contents of his Easter basket—mini eggs, gold foil-wrapped chocolate coins—onto her tear-smeared face.

Molly shakes her head to empty the memory and walks faster. She barely notices the sunflower nodding in a big red pot or the cat sitting in a doorway as she passes.

As she rounds a curve on the upward climbing street, ahead is the neighbor with her little dog, some sort of terrier.

Molly doesn't really know her beyond saying hello. In fact, thinking about it, she hasn't seen the woman in a long time, and wondered if she'd moved away. She calls out, "Hello!"

Molly has decided to invite the woman over for a glass of wine in the evening when it cools down. It gives her a twinge of dim excitement, something to look forward to The thought of yet another day waiting for night then waiting for day again is almost unbearable and she calls out once more, but the woman doesn't turn around.

Molly picks up her pace, puffing as she climbs the steep street to catch up. "Hey, Cora, hi, wait up."

Still, the woman doesn't respond though Molly is no more than six feet behind her now. The woman's dog turns to Molly. "Hey there," she says, reaching forward to pat it. It bares its teeth and Molly quickly draws back her hand. "Cora?" She still doesn't answer even though Molly is almost at her elbow.

Cora shouts, "Go to Hell."

Shocked, Molly recoils from the ferocity in the woman's voice, then sees the shiny white air pods in Cora's ears.

"Drop dead," yells Cora to her phone, walking faster up the street, dragging her dog by the leash behind her.

Molly stops and lowers her face to her own phone, embarrassed. She stays that way in case Cora turns around. Only when the woman and her dog vanish around another bend in the road does Molly continue her upward climb. It's so hot. She passes a tangle of brittle yellow vines and shriveled tomatoes—someone's attempt at gardening. Dead grass crackles and turns to dust when Molly steps on it.

VII

Where has she gotten to? She doesn't recognize this street. She checks her phone for her location. Without touching it, the screen is already showing her a map with a red marker. Was it always her goal? She doesn't remember inputting it, but shrugs the thought away. She recognizes the location as a place where you can see all the way across the canyon to Griffith Park and beyond to the downtown skyline. An impressive vista. She doesn't recall wanting to get there, but it gives her a goal. Something tugs in the back of her mind. *I'm supposed to get somewhere . . .*

The street grows so vertical it's almost as if she's climbing the side of a mountain. She has to bend down low, almost touch the street with her hands. She can smell the tar melting which reminds her of the stink of the candle in her bedroom. She feel nauseous.

The houses to her left seem to be jiggling like jelly, as if they aren't quite sure if they are really there. It's the heat, hot air distorting her field of vision. "Heat devils," she whispers to herself.

A man with a backpack and an alpine hat suddenly appears up ahead, descending toward her. A puffing Molly pauses her climb, "Was the view worth it?"

The man passes Molly without a glance. Irritating, though not surprising. People she passes these days never seem to smile, don't even return a hello, lost in their own worlds.

A few minutes later a car approaches behind her and Molly steps onto the dirt shoulder to let it pass. She glances over at the slowly cruising convertible Mustang. Tourists always rented convertible Mustangs. The driver is looking at his GPS with a furrowed brow, and the girl beside him says something in German. Molly nods to them, waiting for the driver to ask for directions to the Hollywood sign; readying the standard reply that you can't drive to it, but there are spots to get a great shot. But the driver doesn't seem interested in Molly and presses his foot to the accelerator, causing the car to fishtail.

"Hey!" Molly yells, jumping away from the car. It had almost knocked her into the canyon. The car roars up the street.

VIII

When at last Molly reaches the crest she expects to find the Mustang there as well, but she is the only soul at the end of the vertiginous climb. She's so hot she can feel the burn beneath her skin and she wipes her forehead with her forearm as she surveys the panorama across the canyon to Griffith Observatory and the skyscrapers downtown.

"Oh no." Black smoke is rising in the canyon below. When she holds up her hand to shade her eyes, "What the hell?"

There's a river down there. A band of silvery water winds through the canyon streets below. Which is impossible. The only river within miles is the Los Angeles River and it's not only in another direction, but a feeble excuse for a waterway. The scream of a siren wails, and overhead is the pounding pulse of a helicopter.

Molly looks up, expecting to see either a news crew or a fire chopper, but sees only a crow circling above her head. When she surveys the view again, the observatory, the downtown skyline, are still there, but the serpentine shimmer that looked like a river is gone.

A trick of the eye.

But the fire burning in the distance is no trick. Molly looks down at the tumbling jumble of roofs and roads. The smoke is rising from one of the lowermost neighborhoods in the canyon. Red and orange flames explode in great balls of fire as if blasted by a furious dragon.

Molly is typing on her phone, trying to discover any information about the fire, when she has the sensation that someone else is near. She lifts her head. A man is climbing the street toward where she stands at the hilltop, but where light should be is only a block of dark. Is it heat rising from the street that blurs him? Molly feels something twist in her gut, that feeling that something isn't right about this man. She lowers her face and quickly begins to descend. When she glances up, the man, or the smudged figure, is much closer. She goes cold inside and turns her head away. *Wrong.* The man doesn't seem to have feet. He isn't walking, he is drifting toward her as if windblown.

Sun in my eyes.

But she doesn't look at him. She senses rather than sees that the man has passed by. He is behind her now, climbing the hill to where she was a moment ago. Her skin prickles. *Who was that?* Something tells her not to turn around, not to even to look over her shoulder. *What was that?*

She walks downhill as fast as she can, if she runs, she'll tumble down the hill, break a bone. *Jill came tumbling after . . .*

The sky is growing dark as smoke from the fire below obscures the sun. A hot wind gusts. When she licks her lips she tastes ash.

The sky is rouged red. She is astonished at how fast the fire must be advancing to light the sky like this. The road is no longer so steep, it evens out and Molly breaks into a jog, *got to get home, get the cat get the car get out,* remembering horror stories of people trying to flee a tsunami of roiling flames only to be found later, burnt hands still on the steering wheel, the melted metal tags of their pets inside the skeleton of a car.

She stops a moment to check her phone. She types in the call letters of the local TV station. The screen is fire red, but there is no text. Above Molly's head, the sun is a faded disc, pale as the full moon in the early morning sky. A whoosh of wind blows her backward, strong enough to make her totter. She senses, rather than sees, the shadowy blur of a big dog as it rushes past.

By the time she reaches her street, the smoke has cleared and the sky is dotted with stars. Bright hot and white they flare in the smudged black sky. The moon hangs lopsided as a drunk overhead. The smell of smoke and charred wood, of the chemicals used to subdue the fire makes her gag.

A group of people stand in front of the smoldering ruins of a building. A silvery river of water from the firehoses races down the street to a drain.

"What's going on?" Molly asks a man with a baby strapped to his chest. Instead of answering, he turns to the young blonde woman beside him, "Wasn't that building sold a year ago?"

A woman with a terrier on a leash speaks up, "I used to see someone on the balcony sometimes. Was never very friendly."

Molly's heart slips when she spots the man with the alpine hat standing apart from the rest of the crowd, his face in shadow. She feels drawn to him, but as she begins to move toward him, he lifts his head and Molly stops, covering her mouth to keep from screaming. It's Duncan and he is cradling her cat in his arms.

"No, no, he's dead, he died." She is backing away, her ankles splashing in cold water. She backs farther, the water now to her knees. When she turns to run she is in an enormous river tossed with whitecaps. A boat is gliding through the chop almost as if flying. Molly knows the boat is for her.

"Row."

No I can't, no, I can't.

Molly turns, splashing out of the river, onto a muddy bank. Duncan and her neighbors are gone. There is only smoke and heat. She feels hot breath on the back of her legs and she wants to scream when the smoke billows and expands beside her, but her mouth won't open. The cloud of smoke has four legs. Molly can smell the burnt wires in its fur, see the fire in its eyes.

When she is lifted off the ground, she screams so loud it echoes through the canyon. The great dog with Molly between its jaws is running.

Firelight casts shadows, stark and sharp. The smoke dog whips past burning buildings and Molly sees herself, a silhouette with dangling legs, arms flailing.

The river is receding as Molly is carried away, its silvery gleam now far behind.

IX

A grinning moon is pressed against the sky. Duncan snores softly on the pillow beside her and Molly turns her head to his profile. He is outlined in moonlight, still as a marble effigy. She could be dead lying there beside him.

From the Notebook of Gregorey, Keeper of Village Elders Meeting Minutes

~ *Michelle Knudsen*

Friday

Four more headless calves were born this week. After extensive arguing among the village elders and several attempts to interpret the intertwining slug trails in Jonnis's garden, we have determined that the new arrival to our village is a secret sorceress and must be dealt with immediately. Some of us were excited (perhaps too excited, in certain cases, though I will not name names) to unearth the Old Books from their dusty cabinet for the first time in anyone's memory. We spent the afternoon flipping carefully though their pages, looking for guidance.

Friday (later)

It is worse than we thought. We went as a group (Edmund, Jonnis, Old Knickenbocker, Percival the Younger, Tall Steven, and myself) to confront the young woman, who greeted us at her door wearing a blue dress and a bright smile. "Confess, Magic-User!" we demanded, nearly in unison, as the Old Books suggested, but she refused, insisting she was only a simple seamstress and also that her name was Melanie. She offered us sweet tea but we were too wise to be taken in by her tricks. We demanded her confession several more times, with ever-increasing volume, but she would not be moved. Eventually we didn't know what else to do, so we all went home. In our defense, it should be noted that none of us have actual field experience dealing with sorceresses, and the Old Books' entries on the matter were rather limited.

Tuesday

We debated over the long weekend and finally agreed on the next course of action. Tall Steven was sent to fetch the woman, and the entire village population congregated in the market square. Edmund addressed her as head elder. "Once again, we accuse you of being a sorceress! What say you, stranger to our village?"

The woman once more denied the charges. "My name is Melanie, and I am a seamstress, not a sorceress. If anyone is need of mending or hemming or the like, please come visit me at my home by the river! I offer fair prices and free adjustments if you're not satisfied with the initial work."

There was some interested murmuring from the crowd, until Old Knickenbocker cried out, "Enough! Let her say so while she holds the truth stick!"

Silence fell as Percival the Younger approached the woman with the truth stick. She took it in her hands, looking somewhat bemused, and began to repeat, "Fair prices—"

"No, no," Percy whispered. "The part about being a sorceress!"

"I am not a sorceress," she said.

The silence stretched out. "Behold," Old Knickenbocker said at last, his voice wavering with awe. "She must be a powerful sorceress indeed, to overcome the binding of the truth stick!"

The woman rolled her eyes, handed the truth stick back to Percy, and left the square.

"You cannot fool us!" Old Knickenbocker shouted after her, but she did not turn around.

Tuesday (a different one)

It has been a full month, and we have decided that all we can do is try to avoid antagonizing the sorceress. No more headless calves have been born, so either she has chosen to be merciful or the farm doctor was right about staying away from the sketchy-looking feed-grass by that recently discovered cave in the dark forest. Several villagers have been to see Melanie regarding mending and sewing, purely in hopes of staying on her good side. To be fair, her work has been impressive (no doubt she uses magic needles and similar sorceress tricks).

Friday

No updates on the sorceress (except that someone finally tried her sweet tea, and there were no untoward effects, so now we all drink it when we stop by; it's quite delicious) but that cave in the dark forest seems to be getting bigger? Edmund has sent Percival the Younger and Tall Steven to investigate and report back.

Saturday

Percy and Steve never came back last night. Can't write more; must help search.

Saturday (later)

We found them, but they are in rough shape. Percy still hasn't said a word; he only shakes and trembles and huddles in his infirmary bed. Tall Steven is missing two-thirds of his left arm. He cannot recall how it happened. The wound, in some small gift of grace, is perfectly cauterized, so he did not die from loss of blood. He remembers approaching the cave, which did indeed look bigger than the last time he'd seen it, and stepping into the darkness. Then there are only flashes: a sudden numbing coldness, seven floating shapes that he insists were the heads of all those poor headless calves, a pair of glowing crimson eyes.

Jonnis has gone to fetch the sorceress.

Saturday (later still)

She refuses to help us. Even now, she holds to her seamstress story and claims she has no magic to fight whatever is living in that cave. She did come to visit the infirmary with some sweet tea and two beautifully knitted blue blankets, and her presence had a calming effect on Percy. He has stopped shaking and was even able to sit up a little to drink the tea. The rest of us are furious, however. We have granted her every courtesy and haven't persecuted her or *anything* and now in our hour of need she turns her back. I may never wear those pants she hemmed for me ever again.

Sunday

Old Knickenbocker wants to offer the sorceress as a sacrifice to the cave-creature in hopes of placating it. I am uneasy about this idea, to say the least, and Percy (who is much better today) flat-out refuses to allow it, so there is little chance Old Knick will get the unanimous vote required for such an act. We must do something, though. Several other villagers have now seen glimpses of the floating shapes at the edges of the forest, and it seems pretty clear that this can't mean anything good.

Sunday night or maybe early Monday

I cannot sleep. My mind is full of visions of disembodied calf heads and eyes the color of blood. I walked down to the river, partly to try to clear my head and partly because I had half-formed notions of pounding on Melanie's door until she awoke and then threatening or maybe begging until she agreed to come to our aid. When I neared her home, however, I saw that there would be no need to wake her. I could see her through the window in the soft glow of candle-lamps. She was seated at her kitchen table, her head bowed, her hands covering her face. She may have been praying, or pondering, or crying. I could not bring myself to disturb her.

Monday

Percy burst in to the morning meeting just as we were about to begin without him, shouting that Melanie was gone. We followed him to her house, where we found only a pile of completed sewing projects and several pitchers of sweet tea. We looked at one another, then slowly turned toward the forest. Percy took off at a run, and the rest of us followed him again. Several other villagers saw us and followed in turn.

When we reached the cave, we found the seven calf heads neatly arranged in a half circle on the ground, each impaled with a knitting needle that pinned it to the earth. Visible just inside the cave mouth was the head of a monstrous creature, the like of which I have never seen nor imagined, its gray, barklike skin pierced by what seemed a thousand tiny needles. Its eyes were sewn shut with bright blue thread, and sticky black blood trailed from its misshapen ears and pooled around its head on the cave floor.

Just beside the dead monster, a single sewing needle hovered shakily, point down. As we watched, it dipped its point in the pool of blood and then scratched pen-like across the ground, tracing the word *farewell*. Percy fell to his knees with a moan. I placed a hand on his shoulder, trying to contain my own confused emotions. She had saved us after all, been sacrificed after all, been a sorceress after all, and a seamstress too. I suspect the first and last of those were all she'd ever really wanted.

Tuesday

We renamed the dark forest after her, by unanimous vote. It's full of flowers now. All of them are blue.

KNIGHT of WANDS.

There Be Dragons

~ Ingrid Garcia

—*The Flight Forward*—

Marta Lopez moved to her seat preoccupied, her thoughts racing so hard she bumped into the Rastafarian gentleman who was putting his bag in the overhead bin of the adjacent seat.

"Sorry," she said, "my mind's in such a weird place, I forget about my surrounds."

"No worries," the tall, dreadlocked black man said, "and I certainly hope it's a good trip."

As the tall black man nodded in agreement, his dreadlocks softly swinging, he flashed a thoughtful smile and said: "by the way, I'm Kai Menelik."

"Marta Lopez," she said, shaking his hand, "Nice to meet you." Marta put her belongings in the luggage bin, taking out her tablet, and sat down. She had a lot to contemplate, wondering if she'd done the right thing. She grabbed her airpods and was about to pop them in her ears when she saw that Kai Menelik was about to do the same. He noticed, too, and laughed. "We're aping each other." He said.

"Yeah," was all she managed, "If you don't mind me asking: how important is music to you?"

It cut dangerously close to the chase. If he knew what she'd done to the music he was about to listen to, he might not be so amused. Thankfully, he couldn't read her mind.

"Very important," he said, pointing to her tablet, "and if you don't mind my curiosity: how important is technology to you?"

"Very important," she said, wondering where this was leading to.

"Could you live without it?" he asked.

"I suppose I could," she said, thinking it over, "but—"

"—it wouldn't be a life worth living," he said, finishing her thoughts.

Yet, there's more to it that that, she thought, *music can be not just the message, but also the prime mover.*

"Suppose music became so powerful, so compelling," she said, "that—for example—people would actually, well, act out John Lennon and Yoko Ono's 'Imagine'?"

"Imagine all the people," he intoned, "really changing the world for the better? More cynical persons would call that hopelessly naïve."

"It would be," she reluctantly admitted, "but suppose there was something in the music that would compel people to behave like that?"

The moment the words leave her mouth she regrets stating them. For Avitome she helped develop the 'best and most affordable DACs in the world'. In her spare time, though, she went much further by inventing a binaural technique that could stimulate carefully selected parts of the brain with certain frequencies. With a revolutionary algorithm she could aim her aural stimulations with pinpoint precision.

That was all within her field. Much more challenging—for her—was to find out which parts of the brain to stimulate, and to what effect. Until she was put on the right track by ground-breaking research and found a way to impel curiosity in the brain, a way to instill an insatiable thirst for knowledge compelling people to become a vector for change—say a scientist, engineer, entrepreneur or volunteer.

She secretly developed BAD-ASS—her Bin-Aural Deep-Algorithm Stimulation System—that could be embedded in a song, *any* song. The binaural tones were inaudible for anybody and anything but the finest audio analysis equipment. Hacking into popular music streams like Spotify, Google Play, Pandora and Apple Music she converted their most popular songs into the BAD-ASS enhanced ones.

She finished the hacks yesterday, before heading for the Shanghai International Audio Show.

"That might help," Menelik said, "but I suspect people are also motivated by fear, jealousy and greed, probably in that order. What about if we eliminated those?"

"That could be good," Marta said, "but—like love, compassion and joy—I think these are deep-seated emotions, ingrained by evolution."

"I don't want to eliminate these emotions," Menelik said, flashing a broad smile, "I want to eliminate the *need* for them."

They talked in strangely hushed tones, as if afraid other passengers would overhear them, yet secretly wishing everybody would listen. "Technology is basically a tool, albeit a stupendously advanced one," she said, "and it's the people using it that determine if it's used in benevolent ways or not."

"That might be true now," he said, "but what if technology develops so much that it frees us from wanting, that it can provide us with anything we need, for a price too cheap to charge?"

By now, Menelik wondered if he'd said too much. On the one hand, he'd safely cached the encrypted blueprints for the self-repairing nanotechnology he'd developed using the massive resources of MIT's Media Lab, telling his director Joi Ito that his approach was a 'forever-shifting approach to the ideal'—self-repairing nanotechnology that could be adapted for any possible use—while admitting they would never ever reach that veritable point of perfection.

Problem being that one evening, after experimenting all day with one extremely experimental amplitudron-encoded structures, the prototypes started working so well, so eloquently, so effortlessly that Menelik feared he'd actually achieved it. Working through the night, he threw tasks at the novo-prototypes that he'd considered impossible to achieve. Yet his new machines succeeded beyond his wildest dreams.

Then he wrote down the blueprint for his novo-prototypes, encrypted them and put them on several secret caches in the cloud, programming their release—ensuring they'd be both open source and public domain through a carefully crafted legal document preventing that other could retro-actively patent them—in case of his death or disappearance.

Machines that can be programmed to make anything—almost literally anything—needing only the raw materials and energy. The former could be recycled through his novo-prototypes, and the latter was only a matter of manufacturing sufficient renewables—hell, these machines could make their own solar- , geo- or wind power converters.

It could trigger the advent of a post-scarcity society. If everything could be made so cheap it would be pointless to charge for it, then greed, jealousy and even fear—the fear of poverty and destitution—would become obsolete.

Still, Menelik wasn't sure what to do. He could show it to his peers, but was afraid they'd cripple or destroy the technology for a variety of reasons—safety, massive disruption, possibly mis- or malevolent uses. He could go public and face a tsunami of controversy. He just didn't know, so he decided to put it on hold after he returned from his trip to the Nano Tech China Exhibition & Conference in Shanghai.

He could not just spill these beans to the first stranger he met on the plane—no matter how cute, smart and tech-savvy she appeared to be. Yet, by dog, he did need to exchange viewpoints with another intelligent, like-minded human being, and she did seem to fit the bill to a T.

So they kept talking possible scenarios for change in general terms, carefully avoiding telling details. Their animated discussion was interrupted by the meal service. Yet the exchange was so engrossing and invigorating that Marta almost forgot about her environment. Some nagging doubts came up, but she discarded them as fatigue set in, and she decided to take a nap.

She slept well, rarely slept so well in a plane before. And it was so quiet that, as she was awakened by a slight bump—almost like a wrinkle in time—and the sound of a cough from someone in one of the seats behind her, she almost feared that the engines had stopped. But no, they were still flying, albeit in near silence. Wasn't there much more background noise, normally?

She looked out of the window at the left wing. It seemed much sleeker than when they took off, but she must be imagining it. And the windows—they seemed much bigger, too. Strange, but she shook it off as their conversation continued.

"Is it me," she said, "or are these engines really so quiet?"

"Well, isn't this a dreamliner?" Menelik said, mistakenly, "but I also didn't realize it would be so well-insulated. Sometimes technology improves faster than you think."

"Indeed," Marta said, "if only people could improve so quickly, as well."

"Imagine that," Menelik says with a dreamy look in his eyes, "the world living as one."

—*Into the Future*—

Arrival augurs future shock. From her window seat, Marta sees a flexible trunk like a giant snake curl its way to the plane's exit door. The crew doesn't open the door, rather it dilates the moment the giant trunk attaches itself to the plane's exterior. Exiting the plane, each passenger enters their own transparent globule, which nictates shut and vacuums each passenger towards their immigration receptacle. Bio-samples are taken so fast and non-intrusively, that both Marta Lopez and Kai Menelik are waived through before they realize they've been tested.

Each immigration receptacle exits into a giant corridor. Next to each exit, a robot arm holds up a plaque with each passenger's name, and several other robot arms proffer a cart holding each passenger's luggage. Baffled, Marta takes her cart and is directed to a moving sidewalk that quickly takes her into the arrivals area. Menelik arrives there at the same time, next to her, looking bewildered, as well.

The arrivals hall is filled to the brim with people who—on closer inspection—each seem to live in a little world of their own. Some gesticulate frenetically, some talk loudly, some move around in state of serenity, yet—as nobody seems to be paying attention to anybody else—nobody bumps into each other, as if some invisible tech bubble protects them. Most of them look strange in a subtle way—their muscular proportions seem off or they carry artificial extensions. Even more disturbingly, there are no signs indicating ground transport, metro links, parking lots or even the exit.

Lopez and Menelik face each other, uncertain what to do. The moment they seem to head somewhere—anywhere—a Chinese person whose androgyny would make David Bowie jealous emerges from the chaotic crowd, heading their way, saying something that sounds like English but is so full of neologisms, jargon and portmanteau words that it might as well have been Mandarin.

"I'm sorry, but I don't understand you," she says, "do you speak English?"

"What's wrong with you two?" The English that seems to appear out of thin air does not synchronize with the speaker's fast-moving lips. "Is your AugRealApp malfunctioning? I pinged you several times."

"My AugRealApp?" Marta says as she takes out her iPhone, checking the App store, "Is that the latest hype?"

The Chinese looks at Marta's iPhone in utter disbelief, then starts laughing uncontrollably. As the laughter subsides, they say: "What's that? A display box? A phone cell or whatever they were called?" They shake their head. "Where are you two from? The Luddite Archipelago? The last remaining Amazon tribe? Anyway, these are useless here. In modern society, you can't get anywhere without ubik-link implants."

"Ubik-links?" Menelik says. "I'm a nerd, utterly up-to-date with the latest shit, and I've never heard of them."

"No problem, dear medieval people," the Chinese says, quickly touching an antenna-like appendage on their head, "I'll set you up."

"Set us up?" Marta says, "I'm not sure if we can pay for that."

"Pay?" The Chinese shrugs. "That's a concept from the Stone Age." They pause and contemplate. "Dear Luddites—I almost forgot people like you still existed—but in our modern, post-scarcity society money has become obsolete. To get around, you need an AugRealApp system, which connects you with the ubik-link."

"But I'm not sure if I want that." Marta protests.

"You can't get out there," the Chinese waves their—weirdly proportioned—arms in all directions, "without an AugRealApp. You'd be run over by an ElectroBus, smashed by a SurfaceZep or chopped up by a HyperDrone, as they can't see you." They sigh in exasperation. "You wouldn't survive ten minutes, out there. Surely you're not *that* stupid, or suicidal?"

"This doesn't make sense," Marta says, "where are we?"

"Über-Shanghai, of course," the Chinese says, their hands operating some invisible interface with blinding speed, "don't tell me you took the wrong flight."

"Über-Shanghai?" Menelik says, frowning, "maybe we should ask what year this is?"

The Chinese rolls their eyes. "Do you have a different calendar, out there in the Luddite Archipelago? It's 2038, of course."

"That's impossible," Marta says, "then we're twenty years into the future."

☉

After they've recovered from their shock, Marta and Menelik check for signals with their smartphones, tablets and laptops. No networks or signs of life anywhere, except for the Homeric laughter of the Chinese as they type on their laptops. With great reluctance, they allow the Chinese person to 'set them up'.

A cloud of insect-like drones—so realistic they're indistinguishable from an actual swarm—descends upon them from somewhere above the huge arrivals hall. The insectoids crawl on their arms, face and under their clothes, weaving in implants everywhere. Especially the eye sensor implantation freaks them out, until they notice the process is completely painless. Either the insectoids work with nano precision—avoiding nerve endings all the time—or they use a highly advanced local anesthetic. In any case, the physical implementation is over in mere minutes.

Just like the semi-autonomous, self-repairing nanobot factories I was foreseeing, back then, Menelik thinks, *this means we're really into the future.*

Then the weirdness begins. . .

Extra sensory perceptions pop up everywhere in their nervous system as the Chinese—Jing Shenteng—moves them around the hall, through the dense, chaotic crowd in order to auto-tune the AugRealApp system. The visual overlays of augmented reality are the most overwhelming and disorienting. But they can't help but notice the subtle controls of their muscles to steer them away from collisions; the calming fragrances of myrrh, lavender and lemongrass; the cacophonous myriad of sounds translated/transformed into an auditory matrix that's almost understandable and the gentle, refreshing taste of tea, chamomile and vanilla on their tongues.

Voices from everywhere/ubiquitous visuals/suffusing smells/palatal effervescence/permeating elation

Look up↑—Look down↓—Look out!—Look around□

It can happen to you—It will happen to you—It has happened to you

It can happen to me—It will happen to me—It has happened to me

It can happen to everyone—It will happen to everyone—It has happened to everyone

Eventually—Inevitably—Irrevocably

We're coaxed into feeling at ease as we get used to this new technology, Marta thinks, *and it works wonderfully. Scary as hell.*

Because they are guided by the AugRealApp—Marta realizes—they can give their full attention to all the augmented reality overlays, which are overwhelming at first. There are at east six different ones in their forward field of vision, all slightly out of focus until you look at one directly, which then becomes razor-sharp and crystal clear. Instant zoom-in action in a bokeh multiverse.

Fragrance is a profuse and mesmerizing bouquet, shifting all the time. Flavor is a bountiful and exquisite feast for the palate, metamorphosing subtly yet endlessly. Air vibrations are omnipresent—an intricate wall of sound layered by nothing but human voices. An a cappella fractal ring referring a fatal carnal palace, exploding from a center and falling back, all the time, in time, timelessly:

We	We	We
Can	Can	Can
	Work	
It	It	It
Out	Out	Out

Then Marta recognizes it: a myriad of voices, overdubbed into an audible eternity, yet placed in precise locations through bin-aural trickery. *The BAD-ASS system I invented,* she realizes, *but then developed to the next stage. Make that stages.*

When zooming in on an overlay, Marta and Menelik are immersed in an augmented reality that feels like equal measures RPG, documentary and advertorial.

- There's Boris the Eco-Warrior who assists in restoring the Amazon rainforest—rewilding the land, re-introducing extinct species or bringing them back from the brink and re-implementing biodiversity, cross-referencing his results with Yuki the Bio-Wizard;

- There's Suzy the Space-Lifter who floats in geo-synchronous orbit, part of the team that designs and manufactures the triple carbon nanotube ribbon that's lowered to the base station while feeding the dreams of Juanito the Master of the Multiverse;

- There's Alex the Zen-Teacher who's immersed in one of the huge neural nets that run the drone, pharmaceutical and self-driving systems, goading them away from catastrophic failures through invisible kōans and the grey box method and feeding their impossible findings to Dewi the Hyper-Transformer;

- There's Yuki the Bio-Wizard, who enchants DNA, RNA and cellular automatons in her fight against all diseases and her search for extreme longevity which then can be used by the interplanetary colonists eventuated by the works of Suzy the Space-Lifter;

- There's Juanito the Master of the Multiverse, who invents, develops and explores an infinity of worlds and possibilities both virtual and augmented, feeding his results to Boris the Eco-Warrior, Suzy the Space-Lifter and Alex the Zen-Master;

- There's Dewi the Hyper-Transformer, who goes to the poisoned places like industrial landfills, nuclear waste dumps and plastic oceans and recycles the pollution into useable materials many of which are shipped to Suzy the Space-Lifter, Boris the Eco-Warrior and Farida the Vertical Farmer;

"What are these interactive . . ."—for lack of a word Marta just points at them—"apps for?"

"Apps?" Shenteng laughs at the parachronism. "They're recruitment virts."

"You mean these RPGs-cum-videos depict actual jobs?" Menelik said. "That's impossible. According to you, we're in 2038, not in 2138."

"Check 'The Shift' on Wikimedia Galactica," Shenteng says, "sometime late 2018/early 2019 things began to shift. Finally, humanity was coming off its lazy ass and started grabbing the future by the horns. Once everybody was truly motivated, things moved really fast."

"Post-scarcity?" Menelik cannot believe it. "In a mere twenty years? And we're building a space elevator? Holy shit!"

"Three space elevators," Shenteng says, "One near Singapore, one at Kobékobe and one west of the Galapagos Archipelago. We've grown up, we demand redundancy. Huge demand for Space Elevator Engineers of all kinds: nanotechnologists, superconducting techs, micro-gravity specialists and many more."

"But it'll take ages and immense efforts just to teach these new skills."

"Education didn't stand still, either," Shenteng says, "We'll have you up-to-date for the required job in six months, a year tops."

"Cyborg enhancements, genetic modifications on demand," Marta notices, "are most of you still human anymore?"

"Unfortunately, quite a few still are," Shenteng says, "as we are becoming more than human. Speaking about that—" he gestures at an overlay, "—our medical nanobots determined quite a few issues with your health. Each of you should get these treated, quick."

"But we can't pay," Marta says, "our money is obsolete."

"It's—" Shenteng pauses as they search for the correct anachronism, "—free. We need healthy people to join our projects. So much to do, so little time."

Something nags at the back of Marta's mind. On top of these highly interactive presentations, Marta gets the ineluctable impression that these people—even if some of the cyborg enhancements and genetic modifications make them look more than human—are in constant touch with each other through their AugRealApps and ubik-links, which also seems to be an entangled social network—always connected, always on, always there.

"This AugRealApp," Marta says, "is it ever really down? Can we switch it off?"

"Switch it off?" Shenteng says, looking flabbergasted, "Why would you do that?"

"Some people might not like it if—search 'George Orwell' on your WikiGalactica—Big Brother is watching them all the time." Menelik says.

"Those can go to the Luddite Archipelago," Shenteng says, "Our hyper-connectivity has made us more aware of each other, more understanding and thus more willing to truly co-operate."

"But what about privacy?"

"Overrated," Shenteng says, "and obsolete."

"And the need to contemplate things alone," Menelik says, "and in silence?"

"There'll be plenty of time for that once we head into space," Shenteng says, "Space is huge and travel speeds are slow. Unfortunately."

"Still, this sounds too good to be true," Marta says, "Surely you do have problems."

"Of course we do," Shenteng says, "and every new solution throws up new challenges. But we know that we can work it out. Will you join us?"

Marta and Menelik don't answer immediately. They're overwhelmed, overloaded, future-shocked even if it's the future they made possible. To succeed beyond your wildest dreams, be careful what you wish for, to boldly go where no man has gone before and other metachronistic clichés.

"It reminds me of the sea charts of yore," Menelik says, "where the unexplored areas were marked with 'There Be Dragons.'"

"I see what you mean," Marta says, "and as our geographical knowledge increases, the areas of 'There Be Dragons' move in time, to the future."

"You old school westerners do really need to know more about other cultures," Shenteng says, "it will tell you that there are two types of mythical dragons. The European kind is an evil, fire-breathing chaos-monger. The Asian one is a benevolent symbol of fertility, associated with water and the heavens. Welcome to 2038."

A Short History of Decay

~ *Matthew Cheney*

Who first named the eastern edge of the city *the flats*, nobody seemed to know. The designation likely dated to the days when the region was all farmland, before the building of the papermill that turned the village into a town, the town into a city. A particularly large and level field could not help calling attention to itself in the hilly landscape. And so, *the flats*. After decades of abandonment, the papermill got demolished twenty-something years ago in a last gasp of hope for the new millennium. But the flats remained.

As Walt looked out at the expanse of rubble and sod, he felt no impulse to seek an early etymology. The name remained an accurate description. Luxury condominiums may have risen recently a mile away, but the field, the derelict buildings, the rutted roads, the tufts of weeds bedeviling crumbled sidewalks—all offered testament to the collapse and neglect that had infected the city for half a century. Here and now, everything in sight was fallen, forgotten, flat.

He had given little thought to why there was a solitary park bench at this corner of the flats. He assumed there were other benches somewhere farther down, though he could not see any. Perhaps there had once been a park here that was maintained by the city, perhaps there had been numerous benches and they had been taken away, their iron and wood repurposed, and this one got forgotten or left in homage to the past, or perhaps it was simply a little too big to fit on the final truck hauling the benches to a more favored location elsewhere. No matter. Speculation is pointless when no answer is possible. The bench was there and he sat each day on it and ate his lunch.

One of the reasons Walt liked this spot for his meagre lunches (peanut butter and jelly sandwich, can of seltzer water) was how abandoned and empty it was. The offices of the regional art museum where he worked were cramped and stuffy. It was nice to be able to get away from people, nice not to feel eyes glaring or questions haunting faces, nice not to wonder what people were thinking about him, or if they were thinking about him. The previous tenant of the little apartment he rented had left behind a tv, and at night Walt watched whatever happened to be on. Recently he had seen, for the first time since childhood, *The Invisible Man*. When Claude Rains unwrapped the bandages covering his face and revealed his invisibility, Walt found himself suddenly sobbing.

For a few days, perhaps a week, he did not notice any other people at the flats. Then, as he stared idly across the field of greenery and ruins, clouds dawdling in the sky, a breeze jostling litter on the ground, his sandwich half eaten in his hand, he saw figures. They were far off, out in the tall grass and shattered cement. How odd to see people in the flats! (Perhaps there had been people on other days and Walt had not noticed them; he could not be sure.) They were just far enough away to be difficult to see in any detail. They hardly moved, just stood out there in the field. Maybe vagabonds, drifters, people unencumbered by deadlines or expectations, no reason to go from one place to another.

Every day that Walt took his lunch out to the flats, he saw the people. They seemed like sculptures at first, like a public art display, or maybe a weird yoga group or practitioners of tai chi. Day by day, almost imperceptibly, the figures moved closer to his side of the flats. He could see that their clothes were dirty, ragged, torn; their faces grimy. They did not interact with each other. Now and then, one of them knelt down in the field and rubbed their hands in the soil, sometimes then bringing their hands to their face. A few even seemed to eat whatever it was they had pulled from the ground. Remembering an exhibition of medieval paintings he had curated early in his career, he began to think of the figures in the field as mendicants. All those paintings titled Man of Sorrows; all those images of naked, suffering men, of flagellants and the glory of pain.

Every couple months, Carlos sent Walt a package with a card from the girls and sometimes some of their drawings, as well as whatever random mail still came to

the house in Walt's name. Occasionally, Carlos added a
brief note of his own. Walt sent a few hundred dollars
in child support every month, even though it was not
required in the divorce agreement. Carlos, who worked
in real estate development and made that much money
every hour or two, told him it was ridiculous and refused
to cash the checks. "There is no need to punish yourself,"
Carlos wrote in one of his notes. Walt sent a brief reply
on office stationary: "I am not punishing myself. I love
the girls. Please deposit my checks."

More and more, Walt wondered if perhaps he should
stop sending checks, maybe even stop opening the
packages Carlos sent. Move on. Forget that old life, be
whoever he was now. Whoever he was now.

He began to rush through his morning work, finding
himself more annoyed than ever before at the
pointlessness of the emails he wrote and the phone
calls he made, the interruptions by staff who needed a
signature on a form or an answer to an obvious question,
the vapid meetings. He would dash from the building at
the moment his lunch hour began, all but running to his
place on the lone park bench. He returned to work a few
minutes late and made his way through the afternoons
distracted and lethargic, his mind always partly back at
the flats. Some days, he walked by the flats after work, but
there were never people there. On weekends, the streets
around the area were busier with pedestrians and families,

and one of the nearby churches offered meals to destitute people who gathered nearby. Walt usually found some excuse to walk through on a Saturday or Sunday, but he only saw the mendicants standing in the field on weekdays during his lunch hour when nobody else was around.

Though he disliked churches and priests and the sanctimoniousness of religion, Walt approached a group of church volunteers one Saturday when he saw them handing out packages of food at the flats. "Do you happen to know anything about the people who are out there on the weekdays?" he asked. "The people who stand out there in the field?"

The volunteers gave him shrugs and perplexed looks. A woman with thin grey hair and skin as wrinkled as rotting fruit said, "Lots of people hiding out. Squatters. They never really finished tearing down the mill. Turned out there was a graveyard there or something, a bunch of old bones, had to get permission to continue. Nobody bothered. The houses for the millworkers are still up all around, abandoned. Rotting away. Police clear the place out now and then, but not enough. Folks wander."

"It seems more regular than wandering," Walt said. "It's every day, rain or shine. They just stand out there."

"We don't really know anything about this place," another volunteer said, a younger woman with bright blue eyes.

"But your church is here," Walt said.

"No," the blue-eyed woman said. "All the churches here are abandoned. We're from the other side of the city."

"The good side of the city," the older woman said.

"Yes," the blue-eyed woman said, smiling. "The good side."

"So, how are you adjusting to life here in the boondocks?" Walt's boss, Kelly, asked.

"Fine, I think," Walt said.

"Finding enough to do?"

"Oh yes."

"Are you going to come to the donor event next month?"

"Do I need to?"

"I think it might be good if you were to interact with more of the donors, patrons, folks in the community."

"Okay."

"I'm sure it was different in your city. You probably had dozens of people and didn't need to get everybody out there schmoozing. But we're so small, it's kind of important."

"Right."

"They will love having a new person to share old stories with. You'll be positively exotic. They'll write us checks just for the novelty of chatting with somebody who hasn't been here since Teddy Roosevelt was president."

"Sure."

"You're like our very own new, living-breathing exhibit piece."

Kelly smiled and slapped Walt on the shoulder, then walked off to whatever it was she did all day. Her background was in business and public relations. When Walt was hired, Kelly said she was excited to have somebody in the office who would know what all the art meant. He suppressed a groan with a forced smile. He had worried about what he had gotten himself into, but it turned out that the three curators were actually quite skilled and simply kept Kelly at as much distance as possible. Walt saw his primary job, in fact, as protecting the curators. These days, that often meant trying to highlight the importance of their work to Kelly, who repeatedly said she did not know why a museum of their size needed more than one curator.

Some nights, he found himself telling an imaginary Carlos about his work day. It was the thing he missed most, that opportunity they had to share the ups and downs of their very different jobs, to get the perspective of somebody who wasn't embroiled in all the personalities and politics. As Walt cooked some spaghetti, he said to the invisible Carlos, "She just doesn't understand that no one person can have expertise in paintings and sculpture and materials and fabric and everything else from the dawn of time till now in every country of the world. Yes, we specialize in some things, but the specialties were not planned, they were just what the museum happened to be able to get collections of a hundred years ago, and she thinks one person ought to be able to know enough to conserve it all and present it all and—"

He stared at the boiling water on the stove.

"I'm talking to myself," he said. He tossed some dry spaghetti into the boiling water.

"You are not here. Just me." He stirred the water around the spaghetti.

"I am talking to myself. I am the only one here." He continued to stir the spaghetti as it softened and swirled through the water.

"This is who I am now."

He turned the stove off and left the spaghetti to disintegrate. He was not hungry. He would watch some TV and hope to fall asleep.

It rained every day for a week. Nonetheless, Walt took his lunch down to the flats each day and sat on the park bench and watched the people in the field. They were now only thirty or forty feet from him. They did not look at him. Mostly, they looked at the ground. Rain soaked the rags they wore and the rags clung to them like irrelevant skin. Dirt dripped down their bodies.

Walt's sandwich got soggy. His seltzer water tasted of dirty clouds.

Before Walt went out on the third day of rain, Kelly said, "You should get an umbrella."

"I don't have enough hands," he said.

She stared at him in the same way she would stare at an abstract painting.

On his first day back to the park bench after the week of rain, Walt thought there were fewer people now than there had been before. Before, their numbers seemed to be ten or maybe twenty. Now, he could count the mendicants with a glance: seven. They stood distant from each other. The closest one was only ten feet or so from Walt. The person looked like a man, though perhaps, Walt thought, it was a woman with short hair and small breasts and thin hips, or perhaps a person for whom gender was not so defined. It did not matter. The person stood there, barely moving, never looking at Walt. They knelt down and ran their hands through the dirty soil. They wiped dirt on their face and in their hair.

"We are beginning to know you." A voice from behind—Walt turned around and saw a tall woman with long hair wearing overalls that were filthy but intact. Heavy work gloves covered her hands.

Walt smiled. He wanted to say something, but all the words in his head sounded false.

"You are seeking something," the woman said.

"Am I?" He had not intended to speak.

"An answer, perhaps."

"I would, yes, like to know," Walt said, "what this"—he gestured to the field—"what it is. What it's for. The why of it."

The woman smiled slyly. "The answer is likely less than you have imagined."

"Answers often are."

"Better not to defile with words. Come tonight. After dark. To the old mill chapel. It's at the other side. You'll see our light."

Before Walt could say anything in response, the woman walked into the field and found a place partway between two other people. She removed her gloves, reached down, and covered her hands with soil. She rubbed the soil over her hair and skin as if she were bathing in it. She stood up then and stared straight ahead at Walt until eventually he broke from her gaze and wandered back to his office in the museum.

Carlos always wanted Walt to go to church with him, and now and then Walt did, but it was invariably uncomfortable. He let the girls go if they wanted, but he and Carlos agreed that they would never be forced to go. There was nothing wrong with Carlos's church—it was one of the very liberal Congregationalist churches with rainbow flags out front—but Walt nonetheless felt overwhelmed with hypocrisy when he was inside during a service. He could not understand how anyone could bring themselves to believe in the stories that were being told, the idea of reality that the congregants shared. He had wanted to ask Carlos about it, to have a real and honest conversation where they could both ask each other the actual questions hiding in the backs of their minds, but he did not dare, because he loved Carlos and he feared that what he might learn would disappoint him or that what Carlos would learn about Walt's own beliefs would horrify him and in some way increase the sense of distance that had been growing between them, the sense of distance that ultimately led to Walt not caring about anything anymore and openly fooling around with Evan (the intern with the magnificent eyes and sensuous lips) and then throwing everything away because nothing, in the end, seemed worth saving.

"What do you actually believe in?" Carlos asked him at the end.

"Entropy," Walt said.

"The heat death of the universe? Everything getting cold? Appropriate."

"It's from Greek," Walt said. "Similar to transformation. Literally: a turning."

"A turning away."

"Everything changes," Walt said. "Everyone."

"Everyone," Carlos said, "goes cold."

After work, Walt drove to the flats and parked near the old chapel, a building only distinguished from the ones around it by a small steeple at the top. The buildings must once have been boarding houses for mill workers. They were boxy wooden structures with decades of dull paint faded or flaking from their clapboards, their stoops and porches sagging. Two balconies with haphazard railings reached across upper windows that were cracked and broken, a few covered with wooden planks. As Walt sat in his car, he watched an old man hobble down the sidewalk. No other cars drove by. No other people appeared.

A dim light flickered in the chapel. Shadows floated across the windows. Walt got out of the car. It was a humid night and a sweet but sickly smell lingered in the air, a scent of rot. As Walt approached the front door of the chapel, he heard soft, murmuring voices.

He opened the door slowly. The air here felt even heavier, more humid. He eased his way into the shadowy room. The only light came from candles at the front, candles of various sizes and shapes, all stuck to what once had been an altar and now was a skeleton of rotting boards pustulent with melted wax. There was no other furniture in the room. People—maybe a dozen—walked slowly around the floor in no particular order or pattern. Each person mumbled or hummed, filling the room with a burbling tone.

The woman from the afternoon appeared at Walt's side. "Thank you for coming," she said quietly.

"What is this?"

"Worship," she said.

"Of what?"

"Come, join us."

She led him in and walked with him.

Soon, he began to feel the rhythm of the group.

And then he noticed that the woman had disappeared, that he was walking with the others in a syncopation he could not have described but nonetheless felt, a movement he had become powerless to stop without, he was certain, the whole group stopping. He discovered, too, that sounds issued from his mouth, low rumbles from his throat. He was intoning with the rest, and the sound was not a type of communication but rather an involuntary action, a byproduct of movement.

Hours and seconds danced together, then lost meaning, disappeared.

He thought of the word *clock* but had no image for it. The word was only sound.

The woman appeared from the shadows at a corner of the room. She carried a large silver platter on which meat, fruit, and vegetables had been heaped indiscriminately. She moved to the center of the room slowly, her arms shaking with the weight of the platter. She knelt down and set the platter of food on the floor.

The rhythm of the walkers changed, a focus shifted, and they all turned and faced the food pile, which Walt vaguely perceived to be not only rancid but shimmering with flies and pulsing with grubs, larva, worms. A foul aroma rose from the platter and spread through the room like smoke. People stepped toward the pile. Despite the noxious scent, Walt felt himself drawn toward it. No-one touched him, and yet he was sure he had no more choice of movement than if he were in a suffocating crowd.

Their murmurs quieted to whispery breaths, a tone now the same as that of the many flies buzzing delightedly over the rot. Each person crouched down, fell to hands and knees, still inching forward, soon pressing against each other uncomfortably, jostling as they made their way toward the putrid mound of meat, vegetables, and viscous fruit. Hunger energized the room.

And yet they did not eat, did not open their mouths. Instead, in ecstasy, they rubbed their faces against the pile of food, their skin and hair smeared with ooze and slop, freckled with flies, maggots crawling across necks, scalps, cheeks, noses, mouths.

One person pulled back from the crowd and cried out in orgasmic joy, then another and another, while other people dove in to take their place. Walt, too, found himself caught in the rapture, pressing his way in, closer—closer—closer—until finally the miasma stung his eyes to tears, his nostrils filled with mucus and with fetid beads of pulp, and then his forehead plunged into the reek and slime, necrotic juice sliding down the sides of his face, insects crawling and biting at his sticky flesh, and he could not stop his hands from grasping at the ever more liquid sludge, bringing it to his face, slathering himself with the glory until he, too, could no longer remain on the floor and his legs shot him upwards and his voice called out with primal ache—and gorged with wonder he exclaimed at the beauty of the all.

Sylvia says her favorite color is blue. Sarah says her favorite color used to be blue but now her favorite color is green. Sylvia says her favorite color is green. Carlos laughs and Walt smiles—

Carlos should really be the one doing the cooking, he's the one who spent a term in culinary school, but he says he loves Walt's cooking. Walt laughs and Carlos looks hurt. "I'm serious," he says—

There was rain in the night but the sun shines in the morning through a water-streaked window in their bedroom. The girls bounce into the room, ready for the day. Carlos groans, wanting more time to sleep. In the window, Walt sees sunlight held by a fading drop of water—

They go on their honeymoon to Hawaii. They learn to snorkel, they try surfing, they sit for long hours on the beach. Their last night, they eat a seven-course dinner at the most expensive restaurant they can find. As they walk into the hotel, Carlos stops. He holds Walt's hands, looks into his eyes. "I love you," Carlos says. "I will always remember this night. Forever." They kiss in the warm darkness—

The woman helped him up. Hours, seconds, days fell like refuse to the floor. He and the woman stood alone in the room.

She shuffled him toward shadows where a door waited. "Where are we going?" he asked quietly.

"You need to speak with the elder acolyte. It is close to transition."

Wooden stairs led to stone steps curling down, arriving in a basement lit with candles, the stone walls and dirt floor heavy with inadvertent sculptures of wax. In the dim light, the ceiling felt both distant and dangerously low. The air hung heavy and still, infused with a stench of sewage, mildew, and smoke.

They came to a bed in a corner. Two people wearing rags, their hair wild and unkempt, sat beside the bed. They stood as the woman and Walt approached.

In the bed, a figure lay unmoving beneath a heavy sheet.

The woman put her hand on Walt's back and pressed him forward. "Go close. Be seen. Hear the whispers."

Walt knelt at the bed and leaned in toward the hairless head of the figure lying there. The body breathed slowly. The head turned and beheld Walt with dark emerald eyes sunken deep in the skull. A voice less than a whisper: "You seek . . ."

"Yes," Walt said.

". . . this . . ."

Walt held the body's hand, a scatter of bones dusted with flesh. Tears washed his cheeks as he waited for more words.

Walt felt something move across his hand. A crawling insect, many-legged, winged. It scuttered toward the elder acolyte's head. Walt saw bubbling movement beneath the sheet. Antennae and mandibles appeared, bodies and wings, countless thread-thin legs.

"The greatest creatures," the desiccated being whispered. "The survivors. The gods. Have arrived."

The people beside the bed stood and helped Walt to his feet. Together, they ascended to the morning while the transmigration continued in glory below.

Walt wondered if Carlos had told his minister about it all, about Walt's straying and his abandonment of the family. He imagined Carlos saying to the minister, "I do not understand how he can just walk away. Did he ever love us? What are we to him?"

Walt ought to call Carlos, or even go back to the city and see him, see the girls, try to clear some things up. But what could he say? *You are and always will be my family. Yes, I love you. All of you. But—*

His instinct was to say, *But not enough*, and yet he wondered if the true words were, in fact: *But too much*.

"Did something die in a garbage can or something?" Kelly asked from the corridor. She stuck her head into Walt's office. "Is it coming from in here? Do you smell that?"

"No," Walt said. "All is good." He smiled beatifically.

Kelly stared at him. "You need a haircut. And, if I may be frank, some new clothes? You look like a hobo. Christ, the donor dinner is tomorrow. Get your shit together."

Walt continued to smile.

Only three people stood in the field. Walt did not feel compelled to join them, but he wondered if he should. Perhaps it would satisfy his craving. He reached down near the park bench and grabbed dirt with his hand. He held the hand to his nose, rubbed some of the dirt on his cheeks and lips, tasted it. It was not enough.

He found his way down into the field. In between the other people, he knelt and plunged his hands into the soil. A dark richness to the soil here. Worms undulated just beneath the surface. Below, he knew, though he did not know how he came to this knowledge, the gods were still transforming the elder acolyte, as they had done for countless others and would do one day for himself, if he maintained his faith. His bones would then be brought to the catacombs directly beneath him, the catacombs which had been a burial ground for the mills, though that was hardly when burials here began.

He washed his face with dirt. He spread soil through his hair. He scoured his arms and legs and feet and hands with damp dust of all that had once been something and was no more itself. He stood in the soft sunlight and let the air mingle with his scent and shape and being. The ants and beetles that crawled on him also crawled on the other people standing here, and crawled over all who had been here before.

For the first time in many months, he wished Carlos and the girls could be with him. He wished they could feel the beauty. This was love, true love, the strong love born of connection and unity, of life itself.

Standing still, he imagined what he would soon do, the long drive back to the city where Carlos and the twins waited, and he imagined the wonder with which they would perceive him, the new acolyte. He envisioned the love they would feel once he brought them to a place of rich soil and served them a feast honoring decay, and he imagined their love as they observed him become ready for the gods to give his body purpose and meaning. He saw now in the bright blue sky the faces of his loved ones shining smiles upon him, while in the catacombs below, the gods scurried and swarmed, rendering flesh, cleaning bone, proceeding with the duty which was their desire, the reunion of life and death.

Clouds darkened the sky. Walt looked around and saw that he had been joined by other figures. They moved closer, slowly, in unison. Low murmurs resonated from his chest, throat, mouth.

The woman arrived first. "Welcome," she said.

She held her hand to his cheek. He felt a tickle, then a bite. She took her hand away.

Mendicants approached and one by one made offerings with hands holding gods. They touched his face and hair, they opened his shirt and touched his chest, they unbuttoned his pants and touched his hips, legs, groin. People continued to arrive, continued to bring welcome to him until twilight faded to darkness while he stood in the center of the field, the sacred expanse, stood there garbed by gods wriggling and scampering, raising their wings, quivering their legs, running feelers to and fro, cutting hair and flesh with mandibles, laying new life in pores and wounds. He began to exclaim his joy, but the sound was muffled, muted by the holiness crawling its way down his throat.

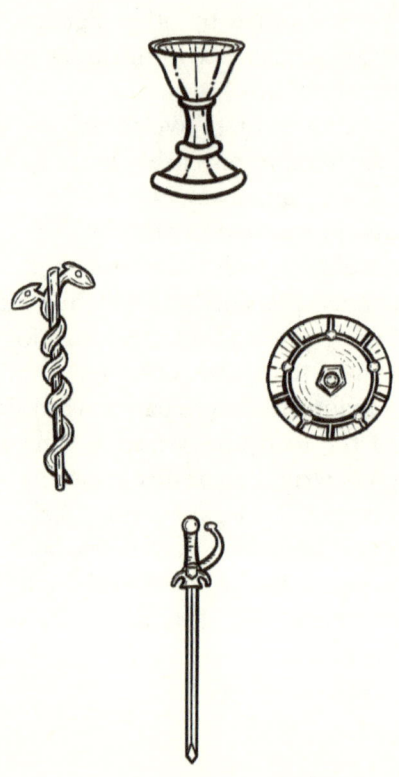

CONTRIBUTORS

Warren Benedetto

Warren Benedetto writes dark fiction about horrible people, horrible places, and horrible things. He is an award-winning author and a full member of the SFWA. His stories have appeared in publications such as *Dark Matter Magazine, Fantasy Magazine*, and *The Dread Machine*; on podcasts such as *The NoSleep Podcast, Tales to Terrify*, and *The Creepy Podcast*; and in anthologies from Apex Magazine, Tenebrous Press, Eerie River Publishing, and more. He also works in the video game industry, where he holds 35+ patents for video game technology.

For more information, visit warrenbenedetto.com and follow @ warrenbenedetto on Twitter and Instagram.

Matthew Cheney

Matthew Cheney is the author of the collections *The Last Vanishing Man and Other Stories* (Third Man Books, 2023) and *Blood: Stories* (Black Lawrence Press, 2016) as well as *About That Life: Barry Lopez and the Art of Community* (Punctum Books, 2023) and *Modernist Crisis and the Pedagogy of Form* (Bloomsbury, 2020). His stories have been published by *Conjunctions, Nightmare, The Dark, One Story, Weird Tales*, and elsewhere.

He lives in New Hampshire, where he works at Plymouth State University.

Sarina Dorie

Sarina Dorie has sold over 200 short stories to markets like *Analog, Daily Science Fiction, Fantasy Magazine*, and the *Magazine of*

Fantasy & Science Fiction. She has published over ninety books, including her bestselling series, *Womby's School for Wayward Witches.*

A few of her favorite things include: gluten-free brownies (not necessarily glutton-free), *Star Trek*, steampunk, fairies, Severus Snape, and Mr. Darcy. She lives with twenty-three hypoallergenic fur babies, by which she means tribbles. By the time you finish reading this bio, there will be twenty-seven.

You can find info about her short stories and novels on her website: www.sarinadorie.com

H. L. Fullerton

H. L. Fullerton writes fiction—mostly speculative, occasionally about being haunted—which can be found in more than 60 anthologies and magazines including *Mysterion, Kaleidotrope*, and several issues of *Underland Arcana*, and is the author of the somewhat haunting novella: *The Boy Who Was Mistaken for a Fairy King.*

You may follow them on Twitter at @ByHLFullerton

Ingrid Garcia

Ingrid Garcia help to sell local wines in a vintage wine shop in Cádiz, and writes speculative fiction in her spare time. For years, she was unpublished. But to her utter surprise—after years of receiving nothing but rejections—she's sold stories to *The Magazine of Fantasy & Science Fiction,* and the *Ride the Star Wind* and *Sword and Sonnet* anthologies, amongst others.

She can be found on Twitter (@ingridgarcia253) and is busy setting up a website.

Elad Haber

Elad Haber has been quietly publishing short fiction for twenty years. He attended Clarion when he was just eighteen years old. You might find his stories in various forgotten corners of the Internet or in the dusty backrooms of basement bookstores. He has forthcoming publications from *Lightspeed, Space & Time Magazine*, and the *Simultaneous Times Podcast*. This is his second appearance in *Underland Arcana*.

Visit eladhaber.wordpress.com for links.

Frances Lu-Pai Ippolito

Frances Lu-Pai Ippolito (she/her) is a Chinese American writer in Portland, Oregon. Her writing has appeared or is forthcoming in *Nailed Magazine, Buckman Journal,* Flame Tree Press's *Asian Ghost Stories*, Strangehouse's *Chromophobia, Startling Stories*, Not a Pipe's *Stories Within, Mother: Tales of Love and Terror, Death's Garden Revisited*, and *Unquiet Spirits: Essays by Asian Women in Horror.* Frances also co-chairs the Young Willamette Writers program that provides free writing classes for high school and middle school students.

K. Wallace King

K. Wallace King has been hired as a screenwriter, teacher, bartender, paralegal, and by her late father, who fired her before her first week was out. Her most recent short fiction has appeared or is upcoming, in *Nightscript VIII, Chthonic Matter*, and *Aseptic and Faintly Sadistic*, an Anthology of Hysteria Fiction. She lives in Hollywood, California, where the hands of dead dreamers are pressed into the sidewalks.

Michelle Knudsen

Michelle Knudsen is a New York Times best-selling author of fifty books for kids and teenagers, including the award-winning picture book *Library Lion*, which has been translated into nineteen languages and was named one of *Time* magazine's 100 Best Children's Books of All Time. Her middle grade fantasy and young adult horror-comedy-musical-theater-romance novels have won honors including VOYA Top Shelf Fiction for Middle School Readers, YALSA Best Fiction for Young Adults, and the Sid Fleischman Humor Award. Her next book involves a giant spider mistaken for a kitten. She also sometimes writes for adults.

Michelle teaches writing in Lesley University's low-residency MFA program, where she is currently the Writing for Young People genre chair. She lives with her family in Brooklyn, New York.

You can find her on Twitter at @michelleknudsen, on Instagram at @michelle.knudsen, or at her website: michelleknudsen.com.

Jennifer Worrell

Jennifer Worrell (she) works in a private university library in Chicago. Her debut novel, *Edge of Sundown*, was released November 2020 by Darkstroke Books. Her short prose and essays appear in *Across the Margin, Write City Magazine, Writing Disorder, Raconteur,* and *Little Old Lady Comedy*, among others.

More information is available on her website, http://jenniferworrellwrites.com. You can find her on twitter (@JWorrellWrites).

PAMELA COLMAN SMITH

The tarot images in this issue of Arcana are from the deck illustrated by Pamela Colman Smith. It was released in 1909 as the Rider-Waite deck (so named, at that time, in reference to its publisher, William Rider & Son). It remains the most influential and widely used tarot deck. While the impetus for the deck came from Arthur Edward Waite, Colman Smith was responsible for the iconography of the cards.

Pamela Colman Smith also illustrated over twenty books, wrote two collections of Jamaican folklore, edited two magazines, and ran the Green Sheaf Press, a small press devoted to women writers. She continued to write and illustrate throughout her life.

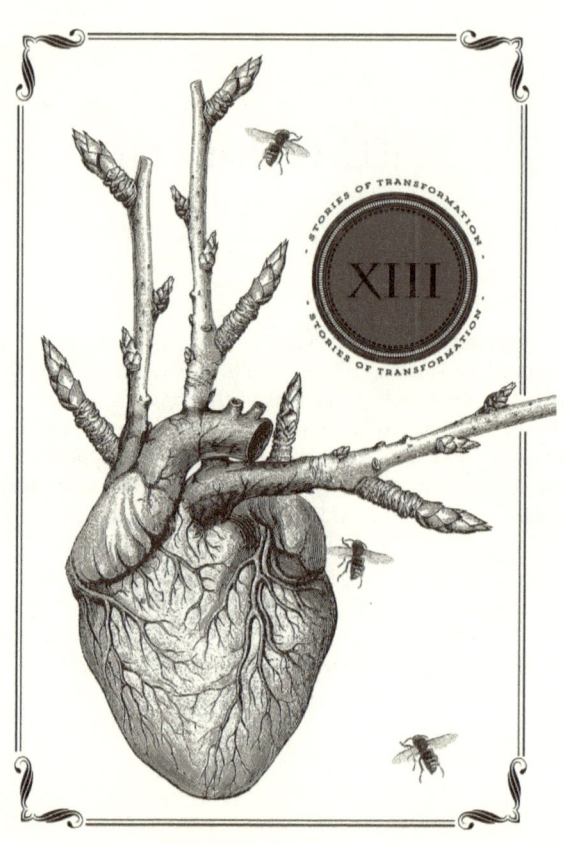

STORIES OF TRANSFORMATION

XIII

STORIES OF TRANSFORMATION

XIII

The thirteenth Tarot card is Death, and he is a symbol not of the end, but of transformation and rebirth. This is the genesis and root of *Thirteen: Stories of Transformation*. The twenty-eight authors of this collection are voices—new and old—who are not afraid to explore what comes next. Whether it be a life after death, a life without love, a life filled with hunger, or the life shared by a ghost. These are stories of the weird, the mythic, the fantastic, the futuristic, the supernatural, and the horrific.

With stories by Liz Argall • M. David Blake • Richard Bowes • George Cotronis • Amanda C. Davis • Julie C. Day • Jetse de Vries • Jennifer Giesbrecht • Daryl Gregory • Rik Hoskin • Rebecca Kuder • Claude Lalumière • Marc Levinthal • Grá Linnaea • Alex Dally MacFarlane • Juli Mallett • Lyn McConchie • Fiona Moore • Gregory L. Norris • Adrienne J. Odasso • Cat Rambo • Andrew Penn Romine • David Tallerman • Tais Teng Richard Thomas • Fran Wilde • A. C. Wise • Christie Yant

Edited by Mark Teppo.

Available at independent bookstores everywhere.

http://www.underlandpress.com

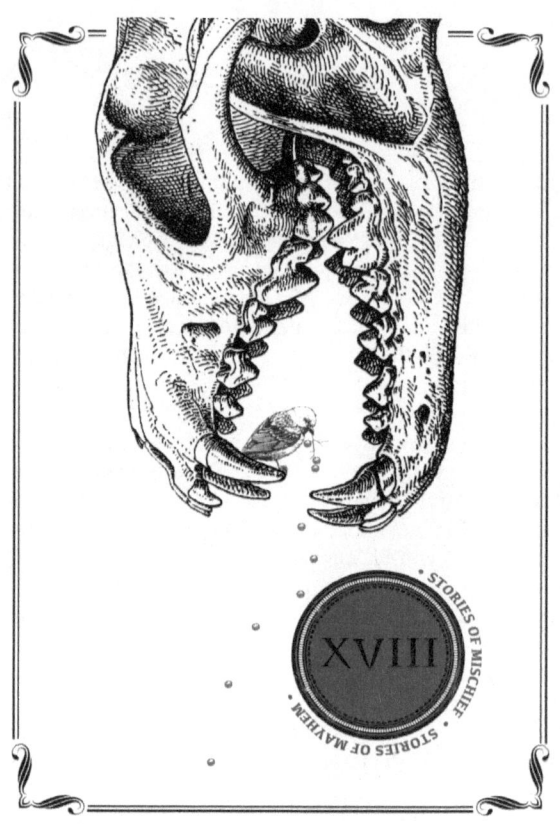

STORIES OF MISCHIEF • STORIES OF MAYHEM •

XVIII

The eighteenth Tarot card is the Moon, and those who raise their arms to her know she offers Mercy and Severity in equal measure. This is the great river at night, where wolves howl and all doors are open. All futures are possible, and every truth is elusive. This is the source and passion of *Eighteen: Stories of Mischief & Mayhem*. These twenty-four stories from voices—old and new—celebrate the inevitability of fate, the horror of prophecy, and the shivering delight of not knowing what comes next.

Cross over the threshold with us, and explore the strange, the weird, and the fantastic. Do not fear what lies ahead. It is the same as what came before. The only difference is you. This is *Eighteen*, and nothing will be the same.

With stories by Forrest Aguirre • Darin Bradley • Christopher East • Scott Edelman • Nicole Feldringer • Ben Gamblin • Ingrid Garcia • A. P. Howell • Emma Johnson-Rivard • E. E. King • Jessie Kwak • Shannon Lawrence • Gerri Leen • Mark Mills • Christi Nogle Tammie Painter • Josh Rountree • Erica Sage • Lorraine Schein • J. Dee Stanley • Richard Thomas • John Waterfall • Wendy N. Wagner • Todd Zack

Edited by Mark Teppo.

Available at independent bookstores everywhere.

http://www.underlandpress.com

www.ingramcontent.com/pod-product-compliance
Lightning Source LLC
Chambersburg PA
CBHW050339110726
47899CB00007B/2563